"You don't have to be scared of me."

But Eloise was scared as Greg put a hand on her arm and continued tenderly. "Let go, darling, let go."

"So that I can have my heart trampled on all over again?" Eloise demanded scornfully. "I could swap memories with you. Memories of a man who said he loved me, who said he'd always be there when I needed him.... And I have other memories...." She blinked away tears.

"Eloise, I'm sorry."

"Yes," she said shakily. "You wanted me to remember the nice things—the kisses and the wine. Well, I remember those, too. But unfortunately one doesn't cancel out the other."

"I didn't suppose it could," he said quietly. "But this time could be different. New memories, good ones, could outweigh the others...."

DAPHNE CLAIR, a fourth-generation New Zealander, lives with her family of five in the sub-tropical area known as "The Winterless North." In addition to her contemporary romances, she writes poetry, historical novels under various names and has won literary prizes for her short stories. About three times a year she tutors courses to help other writers develop their craft. She says she hates windy days, shopping, daylight saving time, prickly plants and having her photograph taken.

Books by Daphne Clair

DAPHNE CLAIR

no winner

Harlequin Books

TORONTO • NEW YORK • LONDON
AMSTERDAM • PARIS • SYDNEY • HAMBURG
STOCKHOLM • ATHENS • TOKYO • MILAN

Harlequin Presents first edition August 1988
ISBN 0-373-11096-0

Original hardcover edition published in 1987
by Mills & Boon Limited

CHAPTER ONE

THE party had not been a success for Eloise. Half-way through the evening she had begged a shirt from Aaron's wardrobe to slip over her dress. 'I didn't know you were having a barbecue,' she said, apologising for taking him away from his guests. 'I didn't bring a jacket.' Most of the party was happening outside, and although it was a pleasant summer evening she had grown too cool in her slim-fitting white shift with narrow shoulder straps.

Aaron produced a white silk shirt with a fine gold stripe that matched the three gold chains about her neck.

'Looks better on you than it ever did on me,' he told her generously as she rolled the sleeves to her elbows and flipped her fair hair over the collar at the back. 'Enjoying yourself?'

She said yes, lying for his sake, and Aaron kissed her cheek and put his arm about her shoulder to steer her back to the laughing, chattering crowd outside. He had soon left her, playing his role as host, and she spent a couple of hours politely listening to pseudo-intellectual conversations in which phrases like 'the kineticism of the whole eighties art movement' and 'the parameters of the ante-post-modernism' were tossed about with gay insouciance, and making small talk with a few bewildered-looking souls who seemed to have strayed into the wrong party. Although she was a fully paid-up member of the Society of Literary and Visual Arts, whose Christmas gathering this nominally was, Eloise sympathised with the wives and boyfriends who had been brought along and deserted by partners now deep in shop-talk with apparently kindred spirits.

By eleven-thirty she had drunk more than she usually did, out of sheer boredom. There seemed to be a lot more drink than food, and she had refused the barbecued lamb, feeling stupidly squeamish after several hours of seeing the carcass slowly revolving on a spit over a fire-pit.

Glass in hand, she leaned against a drunken-looking city-bred totara tree hung with coloured lights, watching the thrice-divorced president of the society skilfully fascinating a pretty blonde who was probably half his age. She was wondering if she could decently leave, when a chorus of voices shouted, 'Hey, Greg!' 'It's Greg!' 'Hey look—Greg's back!'

Before she had even turned to see the new arrival, the party seemed to have shifted in his direction. The president left the little blonde with her admiring smile still fixed on the place where he had been, and bounded across the brick-paved patio to slap Greg on the back and demand to know why Aaron hadn't provided him with a drink yet.

'Steady on,' said Greg, laughing. 'I've only just arrived!'

He was tall, and the light from the open doorway of the house made a narrow gold nimbus about a dark head. Eloise could scarcely see his face against the light, but as she stared across the people crowding about him, he seemed to look up, straight at her. As someone threw a piece of tea-tree on to the dying fire, an amber flame suddenly lit his eyes, making them glow briefly in a strangely frightening way. She felt the drink shake in her hand, and tightened her grip on the glass. Her throat momentarily blocked.

Someone moved across in front of him to hand him a

drink, and she told herself she had imagined it, imagined his catching her eye, imagined her own reaction.

A voice said, 'Is there any of that lamb left? You've got to have some, Greg, the flavour is out of this world ...' And they were moving with him down the slight grassy slope to the firepit, their backs to her. He didn't look round. Eloise pressed back against the tree, willing him to look at her again—telling herself she hoped that he wouldn't.

A young woman wearing green satin trousers and a brief sequined top hooked her arm into his, and he turned to smile down at her, the firelight playing on his face, outlining a dominant, slightly over-long, straight nose and stubborn chin. He bent and kissed her briefly on the mouth. Another woman placed pink-tipped fingers on his shoulder and went on tiptoes to kiss his cheek, and he put his free arm about her. Eloise clamped her teeth tightly as she watched, then finished her drink in one gulp. For a moment she was tempted to try and throw her glass into the firepit, wondering if it would make a satisfactory smashing noise.

The party sounds had swelled with a new note of excitement, and nearby she heard someone say, 'It's Greg Stone, the director—*you* know! He did that marvellous historical film of that nineteenth-century shipwreck, when the Maoris ate the crew and kidnapped the captain's wife.'

'Oh—I saw it! Didn't it have rave reviews in America?'

'And afterwards de Laurentiis or David Lean or someone snapped him up and whisked him off to Hollywood to make films there.'

'Yeah, that's right! Wonder what he's doing back in New Zealand? Holiday, or ...'

Eloise moved away. Her knees felt shaky, and she told

herself she shouldn't have downed that wine with quite
such haste. The patio was relatively empty except for a
small group in one corner who were passing round a
limply rolled cigarette. She had to wiggle through a
crowd of people in the small kitchen, depositing her
glass on the counter. In the hallway she pressed against
the wall to avoid a couple locked obliviously in a
passionate embrace. A little further down, a group of
men were conducting a loud, amiable argument,
liberally laced with unprintable words. She would have
taken a bet that they were writers. It never ceased to
surprise her that so many men whose business was words
seemed unable to find more than one adjective in
conversation.

Aaron's bedroom door was open, and she went in and
pushed it to, muting the sounds from outside. Her pulses
were jumping, her breathing fast. She felt as though she
had been running.

There was a phone by the bed. She sat on the rumpled
imitation tiger-skin bedspread and looked for a telephone book, finding it in a drawer of the bedside table.
She looked up the number for taxis and dialled, only to
be frustrated by an engaged signal.

Trying another number produced the same result.
Her hand was slippery on the ivory-coloured plastic, and
she paused to wipe her palms. Telling herself not to be so
silly, she took a deep breath and lifted the receiver once
more.

She dialled again, and was still holding the receiver to
her ear when the door swung open and Aaron came in.

'Darling!' he said ecstatically, pushing the door
behind him so that it almost shut. 'You're waiting for
me!'

'No such luck,' Eloise said lightly. 'I'm trying to get a
taxi.'

He came and sat beside her, putting an arm about her shoulders. 'You're leaving me already? How could you, Eloise! Eloise—love of my life.'

'Me and a dozen others,' she said mechanically, putting down the phone to fend him off as he tried to gather her into his arms. 'Come on, Aaron, back off. You know it's no good.'

'Hard-hearted Hannah,' he grumbled, but he removed his arms and let her get up. 'You look so sexy wearing my shirt. It's not fair.'

'I was about to take it off, anyway,' she offered, and slipped it from her shoulders.

He groaned theatrically and covered his eyes. Then, removing his hand and assuming an evil leer, he made a lunge for her.

Adroitly avoiding him, the shirt half on and half off, she spun round and saw that the door had been swung wide.

For a moment Greg Stone looked fully at her, and this time there was no mistake. His eyes were blue and blazing, and the full force of them hit her like a punch in the stomach. She gasped.

He said, 'Sorry,' in a deep, clipped voice, then turned on his heel and went away, leaving the door open.

Aaron pulled the shirt over her shoulders again, saying, 'Keep it on, you can give it back to me some other time. I wonder what he wanted?'

'You, probably,' Eloise said, trying to recover her voice. To her annoyance, it shook.

'Really, Eloise dear,' Aaron said reprovingly. 'Even if he's the type, which I doubt—I mean, have you ever seen such rampant virility!—I thought you'd know by now that *I'm* not! Just give me a chance to prove it!'

'You have a disgustingly one-track mind,' she told him, but her heart was not in the banter. Aaron was amusing and harmless and she was fond of him in a friendly way, but now she wanted to get away from him, from the party, from everyone. 'Thanks for a lovely party, Aaron, and for the loan of the shirt. I think I'll walk up to the main road and get a taxi on the rank there.'

'On your own? You can't do that. Wait a bit, I can get you a lift . . .'

'No, really.'

He argued, offered to accompany her, but she refused, managed to slip out when someone called him, and began walking away from the house. The street was lined with parked cars, and the sounds of music and laughter followed her. She had turned the corner towards the main road before she knew she was being followed. And knew it wasn't Aaron.

She quickened her pace, with her eyes on the bright streetlights and passing cars on the road ahead, but the footfalls behind her kept coming, and before she reached the corner they had caught up with her.

She turned swiftly, stepping back, and Greg Stone stopped, watching her rapid breathing, his thumbs thrust into the belt of a pair of dark dress jeans which he wore with a white open-necked shirt. The stance made his shoulders hunch slightly forward, and gave him an air of male aggression.

She felt suddenly dizzy. Too much drink followed by too fast a walk, she told herself.

'Did I frighten you?' he asked abruptly, and then, before she could answer, 'You shouldn't be walking about in the dark alone.'

'I'm only going as far as the nearest taxi stand, and I haven't come to any harm,' Eloise pointed out. 'Unless you're going to turn into a mad rapist.'

Something flickered in his eyes, and his shoulders

went back a little. When he spoke again his voice sounded harsh. 'My car's just over there. I'll drive you home.' He took her arm.

She felt the muscles of her face tauten, and her skin went hot. His expression suddenly became piercingly intent, watching her.

She pulled away. 'I'm all right.' She felt dazed, shocked.

'Sure you are,' he said. 'And I'm driving you.'

This time his grip was firmer, and she realised it would be less than dignified to struggle. It was shattering to realise that one part of her actually wanted to comply. But she said, as he guided her across the road, 'You can't leave the party. You've only just arrived.'

'You noticed?' he enquired with ironic interest.

When he had closed the door on her and then got in himself, she said, 'Everyone must have noticed. You caused quite a fuss.'

'But you didn't join in.' He started the car.

'I was on the point of leaving. And I didn't think you'd even seen me.'

'Such modesty!' He looked at her, and she felt herself go hot all over. 'And it's a lie,' he added casually. 'You knew I'd seen you, all right.'

She sat stiffly beside him, determined not to meet that disturbing gaze again. As the car paused at the junction to the main road, she said, 'I live in Remuera.'

He nodded, and swung the car on to the road. When a little later he turned left at the lights, she reminded him coldly, 'I said Remuera.'

'I know what you said. We're going to my place.'

She drew in a deep, quick breath. 'You can go wherever you please. I'm going home.'

He didn't answer, and when he had to stop again for a

red light she pulled at the handle of her door. It didn't budge.

'You can't open it,' he told her without even looking at her. 'I've locked it from my side. It's electronic.'

She hadn't taken much notice of the car when she got in, only getting an impression of sleek lines and shiny paintwork. But it smelled new and the dashboard was glowing discreetly with green and orange lights, and she realised now that she had seldom had a more comfortable ride. Of course, he could afford the best and latest.

'This is stupid,' she said, her voice brittle. 'You can't kidnap me . . .'

'Don't be so melodramatic. I'm not kidnapping you. And I'm not going to rape you, either.'

'How can I be sure of that?'

He flicked a glance at her. 'I'm telling you, you can count on it.'

'And I'm supposed to take your word?' she asked derisively.

'At the moment, you don't have much choice,' he pointed out.

'What do you want?'

'Now *you're* being stupid.'

She twisted to face him, but he turned his attention back to the road.

'Look, will you please take me home?' she said, keeping her voice carefully reasonable. 'I don't want to go to your place.'

'It's a nice place,' he said. 'You might like it when you get there.'

At his flippant tone, Eloise's patience snapped. 'I don't *care* what sort of place it is! You have no right to take me anywhere against my will!'

He had turned into a side street, and he suddenly drew into the kerb under a giant old plane tree, and stopped the engine. Her hand moved to the door handle, then she remembered that it was locked.

His left hand reached out and flicked her hair back gently where it had fallen across her shoulder. His fingers curled and barely touched her cheek, as he moved them in a slight, gentle caress. His eyes held a question. She couldn't look away, fighting an incredible urge to turn her cheek into his palm.

His fingers were still warm on her skin, gliding from her cheek to the line of her jaw, then up to outline her ear. 'Against your will?' he repeated softly. The questioning look was still there, but there was also knowledge—and a warmth that found an answering spark in her.

Eloise forced herself to turn her head away, rejecting him. 'Don't touch me!' she said, her voice muffled. 'Leave me alone.'

She saw his hand reach out again, making to turn her towards him, and she lashed out, the edge of her palm connecting with his wrist. Glaring at him, she saw that she had roused his temper—and that beneath the temper was another, barely concealed emotion. She shifted nervously.

He flicked his safety belt out of the way, and then pushed the catch of hers. The wide strap rolled silently into its housing. His hands closed over her shoulders and then slid down her back.

She put her hands flat against his chest, trying to hold him off. Her blood was singing through her veins, her pulses racing with a combination of fear and reluctant excitement.

He said again, murmuring the words against the skin of her tautened neck. 'Against your will?' His lips settled just below her ear, warm and questing. For a moment she almost surrendered, then she doubled her hands into fists, but he would allow her no room to attack him. He lifted his head, and one hand tangled in her hair and pulled back her head. For a moment she saw his eyes, gleaming in the darkness.

She whispered, 'Don't!' But he took no notice. His lips barely touched hers at first, but she shivered in his arms, although her body was rigidly resisting. Then his mouth opened over hers, hard, insistent, almost cruel, forcing her lips apart. With shocking immediacy a hot, melting pleasure poured through her, so that her head nestled against his arm, and her spine curved to his embrace.

He kissed her for a long time, and the excitement went on spiralling and spiralling, higher and yet deeper, inescapable, mind-shattering . . .

When he stopped at last he still held her, his lips to her shoulder where he had pushed aside Aaron's shirt, his hair brushing against her jawline and the lobe of her ear. Her eyes were closed, and while one hand was still trapped against the warm beating of his heart, the other had slid about his neck, and was holding tightly to his shoulder.

She stirred tentatively, and he sat back a little, holding her hand in his and bringing it to his lips. He took the tips of her fingers one by one into his mouth, caressing them with his tongue, and sharp little arrows of pleasure stabbed through her, making her breathing uneven, her pulses jump erratically. With their fingers inextricably entwined, he found her mouth again, and this time she was ready for him, meeting him with a little moan, her lips parted and willingly parting further under his determined exploration.

He brought her hand between them again and pressed her palm to the firm, warm flesh where his shirt front was open. Her fingers moved over his skin, under the fabric, and he arched her backwards, Aaron's shirt falling from her shoulders, and the strap of her dress slipping down her arm as he caressed the bared skin gently with his palm. He changed their position, pressing her against the seat back, turning her body under his, then sat up, cursing softly, as his shoulder came in violent contact with the steering wheel.

Still with his arm about her shoulder, he put his lips to her temple and said, with a thread of laughter in his voice, 'We're not a couple of teenagers. This is no place to make love. Let's go.'

He drove slowly for two or three hundred yards, then stopped in a driveway by a house that lay in shadow. They were somewhere in Herne Bay, she thought, near the Harbour Bridge. The faint hum of traffic penetrated into the car. 'Come on, love,' he said, and taking her hand, made to get out.

Eloise had readjusted the shirt and the straps of her dress and smoothed back her tumbled hair. In a shaking voice, she said, 'No.'

Greg turned and looked at her incredulously.

'No,' she repeated in more determined tones. 'I meant what I said.'

His hold on her hand tightened until it hurt. 'I don't believe you,' he said flatly. 'You've just proved that you didn't mean it.'

She took a deep, uneven breath. 'What you want to believe or not is your problem. If you won't take me home, I'll walk to a taxi stand.' She pulled away.

He was silent for long moments, his hands firm on the steering wheel, his eyes looking straight ahead. Then he turned to her and said in a hard voice, 'Who are you being faithful to? Is it Aaron Colfax?''

'What?'

'Is he your boyfriend? Lover? Whatever the term is at the moment?'

'If it's any of your business,' she said coldly, 'no.'

'You looked pretty cosy back at the house. Undressing for him in his bedroom. You should have pulled down the blinds and locked the door.'

'It wasn't what you think. And I don't have to explain to you.'

His hands shot out and grabbed at her arms, holding her in a bruising grip, as though he would have shaken her. His eyes glittered in the darkness, and she heard him draw a sharp breath. She tried to break his hold, but it was useless. He hauled her closer, so that the light from a street lamp fell on her face, her eyes wide and frightened in spite of herself, her skin taut with sudden fear.

A frown appeared between his dark brows, and the expression in his eyes altered from anger to something she couldn't identify. Then he let her go so suddenly that she fell back against the seat. For a few moments he stared at her in silence. Then he turned away from her and started the engine with a roar.

'Tell me what street,' he said.

CHAPTER TWO

ELOISE'S fear quickly changed to a white-hot anger, all the more fierce because most of it was directed against herself, a reaction to the shaming ease with which he had won a response to his kisses.

She was still simmering when he stopped outside her place, a town house in a cul-de-sac behind some of the gracious old villas that lined Remuera Road.

He got out and opened her door, then followed her up the short path.

Taking out her key she said pointedly, 'Goodnight!' then inserted it in the lock and stepped swiftly inside the small entrance hall.

But he was right behind her, closing the door with a click. She rounded on him, her eyes sparkling dangerously.

He leaned back on the wooden panels, folding his arms, a faint smile on his lips. 'Well, go ahead,' he advised her, studying her flushed face and indignantly parted lips. 'You have a choice of clichés. "How dare you?" might be a good one to start with, or, "I don't remember inviting you in", or would you prefer a simple, basic, "Get out"?'

'I was thinking of something even more basic than that,' she flashed. He laughed, and she turned abruptly, putting her bag down on the hall table with the key. Her voice brittle, she said, 'If I give you a cup of coffee, will you go away and leave me alone?'

'That depends.' He was moving away from the door as

she made for the living-room and the kitchen that opened off it.

Eloise paused in the kitchen doorway, warily questioning.

He stood in the middle of the carpet, looking immovable and dangerously masculine, far too sure of himself. 'You might not want me to go, after all.' He quirked a smile at her. Her stomach contracted.

'Don't kid yourself,' she said crisply.

He laughed again, and for a moment she looked at him, the way the laughter creased his tanned cheeks and made his eyes more blue, the way he made everything in the room seem smaller. Then she tore her eyes away and went to make the coffee. The flat felt very warm, and she took off Aaron's shirt and hung it over one of the kitchen chairs.

When she brought in the tray he was standing by her bookcase, holding a hardbacked volume in his hands and studying the photograph on the dust-jacket. 'It doesn't do you justice,' he said, looking at her appraisingly. 'How many books have you had published?'

'Just two,' she answered. She crossed to the low, polished wood table between twin sofas and put down the tray. 'How many films have you had released?'

'A few.' He put the book down beside the tray, reading aloud from the cover, '*No Winners*, by Eloise Dalton.'

Eloise lowered her eyes, experiencing again an echo of the pride and pleasure that she had felt when she first saw her own name on the cover of a book. She didn't want him to see it, to know about her feelings.

'Eloise Dalton,' he said thoughtfully, his eyes on her downbent head.

'Yes.' Silently she indicated one of the sofas. He sat

down and helped himself to sugar. Eloise took her cup and went to sit opposite, but he looked up and said, 'Why don't you sit over here?'

He expected her to refuse. Perversely, she shrugged and sat beside him.

If he was surprised it was quickly masked as he lifted the cup to his lips. She leaned over and poured some cream into her cup and stirred it carefully. He had sunk back into the corner of the sofa, and she felt him watching the movement of her arm as she reached for the cream, the curve of her breast taut beneath the bodice of her dress, the fine gold chains about her neck swaying forward and then settling softly against her skin. She sat nearly on the edge of the sofa, close to the end, not looking at him at all, but conscious of his male presence in a way that made the comfortable, cosy room almost stifling.

'Would you like a chocolate?' she asked him, to break the silence.

'Yes. Will you pass me one, please?'

She picked up the tiny cut glass plate of dinner mints, but he said, 'Just one. In your fingers will do.'

She put the plate back and took one of the small sweet rounds in her fingers and made to hand it to him. But he took her hand in his and carried it to his mouth, taking the chocolate from her with his teeth. His eyes were on her face, but she avoided them and pulled her hand away from his.

'Not for you?' he asked her.

She shook her head.

Greg smiled, but she ignored both the silent innuendo and the way his eyes flicked at her body, making her tingle with awareness. She sipped her coffee, wanting to finish it quickly.

'So Aaron's not your boyfriend?' he said unexpectedly.

'No.'

He looked at her speculatively, as though he doubted her, and she gazed back with defiance. Then he said, 'Do you have one?'

'Do you suppose you have any business asking me that?'

'Eloise,' he said, 'let's skip the games. Is there anyone?'

She hesitated, tempted to make someone up, out of an instinctive conviction that she needed some sort of protection. Perhaps she should have let him think there was something between her and Aaron.

His gaze sharpened. 'Well?'

'No.'

'Has there been anyone?'

'My love-life, or lack of it, is my own affair.'

He laughed softly. 'Bad choice of words, darling.'

She turned her head away, concentrating on her coffee.

'You wouldn't lie to me, would you?' he asked her.

She threw him a glance of contempt. 'Why should I bother?'

He was eyeing her as though he was picking her apart in his mind, going over the pieces. 'So there's no one,' he said. 'Why?'

She forced herself to meet his gaze coolly. 'I've had one bad experience. I don't want to repeat it.'

His eyes were enigmatic, but some spark of emotion—anger or scorn or something else—moved in the blue depths. 'Have you been taking that one bad experience out on all men, ever since?'

Eloise shrugged, forcing herself to hide her own anger

and frustration. He could get under her skin if she let him. She had no intention of allowing that to happen. 'Once bitten ...' she murmured.

'And that's why you changed your mind tonight?' With sudden violence, Greg said, 'For God's sake, surely you could tell this was *different*?'

'Was it?' She felt quite cold now. 'No, I couldn't tell.'

His eyes narrowed on her face. 'That's not true. You're not a fool, and I wouldn't have taken you for a coward, either.'

Eloise decided attack might be the best means of defence. She injected a note of what she hoped was tolerant amusement into her voice. 'What a typically masculine reaction! Calling me names won't get you anywhere. It isn't the first time I've turned a man down, if that's any balm to your ego, and I don't suppose it'll be the last. I'm sorry you've been disappointed, but there were other women at the party who would no doubt have been only too ready to oblige you.'

'Were you jealous?' he asked, an arrested expression in his eyes.

'Don't be ridiculous!'

'*You* were quite willing too, for a while. Don't tell me you weren't keen, back there in the car. I should have followed through then, instead of giving you time to change your mind.' His voice softened. 'I wouldn't have hurt you. I'd make it good for you, Eloise.'

'I'm sure it would have been an unforgettable experience,' she said bitingly. 'I expect you've picked up a wealth of expertise in California. But I'll pass, thanks.'

His laugh was angry. 'What have you been hearing about California?'

'You have just got back from there, haven't you? It's

the fun state, or something, isn't it? The place where all the trends start?'

'You watch too much TV. Actually I was flat-out busy, making films.'

'Yes, you're supposed to be good.'

'I am good,' he said calmly. 'But the competition is fierce, and some of it's good, too. You have to be on your toes. So I wasn't spending my time chasing women on the beaches—or in the bedrooms.'

Eloise finished her coffee and put the cup back on the table. The movement made her shoulder strap slip down her arm, and she hastily started to adjust it, but Greg's hand closed about her wrist, and she looked up apprehensively to see a tight smile on his lips, his eyes gleaming. Her head went up, her mouth firm. Stubbornly, she met his gaze, not unaware of the hostile challenge in hers.

He put his own cup down with a small clatter, and she stood up abruptly, her eyes held by his, her wrist still in his clasp, so that he followed her. His fingers held her firmly, but she felt he was being careful not to grip her hard.

They stood silently, looking at each other, and then his eyes slid over her like a caress. Her physical reaction was immediate and violent, as though he had touched her boldly, intimately. His eyes, with an explicit demand in them, went back to hers, and her pupils dilated, her cheeks on fire. She said on a breath of sound, 'Greg . . .'

His lips barely moved, as he murmured on a note of gentle sarcasm, 'So you do remember my name.'

Tension wove about them, a web of sexual awareness, the air heavy with it. A pulse beat thumped in her throat. 'I don't want you to . . .'

'You *do* want me to. Don't fight it, darling . . . there's no need.'

She tried to shake her head, but the movement was so slight it was almost imperceptible. The golden threads of tension wound tighter and tighter, binding them invisibly, restricting her movements.

He raised his free hand and with one finger slowly pushed up the fallen strap, and the lingering touch sent a lick of fire right through her body. She closed her eyes. '*Don't!*' she begged.

The strap was firmly in place, but his finger traced its line over her skin, from the front of her bodice to the low back, and then his hand flattened on her skin and he said, 'Tell me to go, Eloise, and I will—and I promise I'll never come back. You understand?'

She looked straight into his eyes, her own wide and brilliantly accusing. *Blackmail,* she thought. He'd stooped to that now.

'All or nothing, Eloise. I have to know.' His eyes were hard and bright on hers as he waited for her answer. Abruptly he shifted his grip, holding her face in both his hands, tipping her head back while his eyes bored into hers. 'So, say it—now! Or don't say it at all.'

The anger in her snapped, and she pushed at his hands, raking her nails across his wrists. 'You—you *bastard*, Greg!'

His hands fell away and she hit out at him in blind rage with an open palm, connecting with a stunning force that shocked her and shook him off balance. She saw the reddening mark on his cheek and the promise of certain retribution in his eyes, and knew she had unleashed something in both of them that had been lurking not far from the surface ever since the moment when their eyes had met at the party. She thought she should be frightened, but instead she was filled with a strange exhilaration, knowing suddenly that this confrontation was an inevitable climax to the evening. Her palm stung fierily, and she was glad because his face must feel the same. She had wanted to hurt him. At this moment that didn't even shock her. And she saw that he had been waiting for it, that behind the fury in his eyes was a fierce kind of satisfaction.

Then she was struggling wildly as he swung her off her feet and one sandal went flying. He whirled about and strode into the passageway and found the bedroom door, kicking it open.

Eloise, freeing one hand, doubled it into a fist and aimed for his jaw, but although it numbed her hand, he merely grunted and said harshly, 'Don't ever do that again.

And then he dropped her on the bed, grabbing her when she tried to escape, coming down on top of her, and efficiently imprisoning her flailing arms and legs with his.

She used every ounce of her energy fighting him, and then finally gave up and lay still, panting and resentful, the strange, savage joy of the initial combat rapidly subsiding. His legs felt warm and muscular, wound around her own, the coarse material of his jeans abrasive against the bare skin of her thighs where her dress had ridden up. Her hands were held above her head, and his face was only inches from hers, but she couldn't see his expression because the room was dark. He was breathing hard, his chest rising and falling against her breasts, his weight almost crushing her. She tried to concentrate on that discomfort, rather than the other sensations which were impinging on her mind—but he held her so closely there was no escaping the seduction of the scent of his skin, the heat and the strength of his lean, fit body, the sheer sexual energy that emanated from him. Desire, treacherous, unwanted, stirred in her and then flared, liquid fire in her veins. His head lowered and his face rubbed gently against hers, his lips touching her skin. 'Don't fight me,' he said, his voice muffled against her shoulder. 'Don't, darling, please.'

For a few minutes they lay there, while their breathing slowed, and the silence wrapped about them. Then he shifted, cautiously at first, and sat up. Eloise didn't move, and he began to remove his shirt.

Eloise said flatly, 'I hate you, Greg.'

For just a moment she thought his fingers stilled, then she saw the white blur of his shirt fall to the floor. 'So tell me to go,' he said, and pulled open the buckle of his belt. 'The offer's still open.'

He undressed quickly and came down beside her again, and his leg trapped hers. Her mouth parted, her throat forming the words of rejection, but she couldn't force them through her lips.

His hand touched her arm and ran up its smooth outline. Eloise shivered and averted her head. His palm cradled her cheek and gently turned her. She saw the glitter of his eyes as his head lowered.

'You promised,' she whispered.

'It's mutual, and we both know it,' he answered, 'don't we, Eloise?' Then his lips descended on hers, and she gave a long, shuddering sigh into his mouth, and her hands lifted to caress his naked shoulders and touch the springy softness of his hair.

She woke wearing nothing but the gold chains she had hung about her neck last night before going to the party.

The other side of the bed was empty, and she closed her eyes again quickly, but the images that danced behind her lids were so disturbingly erotic that she hastily opened them again.

Her temples throbbed faintly, and her body ached unfamiliarly and felt sticky. She threw back the sheet and was about to get out when the door opened and Greg came in with a tray holding fruit juice and toast.

His eyes made a lightning, appreciative inspection of her before she drew the sheet hastily back up.

'A bit late for that,' he smiled, putting the tray by the bed.

'I hoped you'd gone,' she snapped.

It was a moment before he straightened and looked at her. The smile had disappeared and his eyes looked quite blank, expressionless. 'Why? Are you expecting someone?'

'No.' She should have said yes, but there was no guarantee that he would go if she had.

He sat down on the bed beside her and handed her the juice. 'Here. It might sweeten your temper.'

'Getting rid of you might do the same.' She took the glass with one hand, trying to hold the sheet with the other.

'Last night I seem to remember you asking me never to go. Stop fiddling with the sheet. You don't need any more covering than those necklaces. I like them.'

He lifted them, letting them drop back against her skin one by one, and then began tracing their curves with his finger. 'I'll buy you another,' he said, 'in remembrance of last night.'

'Stop it,' she said. 'Last night I wasn't myself.'

His fingers twisted suddenly in the chains so that they tightened about her throat, and she caught her breath, afraid he would snap them, or strangle her. His gaze was still lowered, his lids half closed.

'Really?' he murmured, removing his hand and sitting back a little. 'Then who was the passionate lady I slept with?'

Her throat felt very dry. She lifted the glass to her lips and as she tipped back her head saw him watching her, his gaze sweeping the line of her throat, down to the gold chains and the edge of the sheet.

She lowered the glass and he took it from her and picked up a piece of toast. Resolutely, she shook her head. 'I'd like to get up now.'

'So who's stopping you?'

Distinctly, she said, 'Go away.'

'Too late, darling. You should have said it last night.'

'I wish I had!'

'Then why didn't you?'

'I had too much to drink! It's sordid and stupid, but it's the truth.'

'*Is* it?' She had made him angry again, and she felt a peculiar satisfaction in knowing it.

'Yes!' She stared at him defiantly. 'If I'd been in my right mind, I'd never have allowed you in the door.'

'So if you hadn't been drunk . . .'

'I wasn't *drunk*! I had enough to affect my judgement, that's all.'

'How's your judgement this morning, green-eyes?'

It was a trap. She knew it. She stared at him, sensing danger.

'Well?' He leaned closer.

'Go away,' she said. Her voice rose in spite of herself. 'Go away! I don't—I don't ever want to see you again!'

His eyes hardened, boring into hers. He said softly, 'You're scared stiff. Are you afraid I won't take you at your word—or that I will?'

She clenched her teeth. 'I am not afraid.'

'Yes, you are.'

'I wish you'd just——'

'Don't say it again,' he interrupted harshly. His hands grasped her shoulders, and although she moved her head frantically from side to side, trying to avoid him, his mouth found hers and stayed there, stifling her whimpered objections. She expected force, but instead his lips moved coaxingly over hers until her mouth opened under the gentle assault of his tongue, and she moaned deep in her throat. His weight came down on the bed as he sat beside her, and his hands left her shoulders to wander over her skin, touching her throat, and moving down to the edge of the sheet where she was clutching desperately at the white linen.

Deliberately, over her futile resistance, he took her hands in his and spread her arms wide, and his mouth left hers and followed the path of his hands to the curve of her breast above the rapidly slipping sheet.

She made a small, anguished movement and said, her voice half sigh and half muted wail, *'Greg!'*

He laughed a little, and lifted his head. Eloise closed her eyes, trying to gather her will-power, to make some sense of her whirling thoughts. She felt him gather her hair in his hands, and he gently tugged her head back. His lips and his tongue touched her throat, before returning to her mouth. The kiss was a long, drugging, slow experiment, flawlessly seductive. Her resistance gradually melted altogether, until her whole body was one bright, steady flame.

When he lifted his head again, his face was flushed, his eyes alight.

At last he let go her hands and half sat up, his hands

running lightly over her bare shoulders, his eyes commanding. 'Undress me, Eloise,' he said.

Wanting to obey him, her blood raging with need, she bit her lip fiercely with a last, desperate effort at control. 'I don't want you!'

His face changed as he abruptly sat back. His hand snaked down and hauled away the sheet. He looked at her with the most explicit gleam in his eyes, and gave her a glittering, derisive smile.

She flushed wildly, automatically clutching at the sheet to hide from him what he had already seen. Holding it securely, she twisted away, and got off the bed, backing away from him. 'I said no!'

'You certainly exercise your woman's prerogative to the full, don't you?' he said. 'I never knew such a woman for changing her mind.'

'I haven't changed it. I don't want to make love with you. Can't you just accept that you're not God's gift?'

'Last night you had no complaints. In fact, you gave every sign of having a thoroughly good time.'

'All right,' she said, making her voice hard, hoping her eyes would not give her away. 'Last night I was stupid enough to give in to you. Enjoy the memory if you like. Just don't imagine that a one-night stand gives you any rights over me.'

The smile set hard, his teeth coming together. 'OK,' he said. 'I won't. The principle's mutual, of course?'

She shrugged. 'I don't have any claims on you.'

'Right. Your breakfast's going cold.' And he got up and walked out, closing the door with a sharp snap behind him.

Eloise spent several minutes waiting for some further sound, the front door closing, the engine of his car starting up. There was nothing.

At last, she let out a long-held breath and made for the shower.

When she emerged, her hair wet and a towel wrapped around her body, she felt better, but not much. She had just had a sickening thought, and even before dressing she inspected the small flowered calendar that stood on her dressing-table, calculating dates in her head.

She rubbed her hair nearly dry, combed it out and pulled on undies, a pair of jeans and a knitted cotton top.

She wasn't surprised to find Greg in the living-room, but despised herself for the relief she felt at the sight of his dark head bent over the pages of one of her books.

'I don't remember much about last night,' she lied. 'But—you didn't take any precautions, did you?'

He looked up, obviously caught unawares, for a moment quite blank. 'You're not on the Pill?'

'No, actually. I don't *usually* go in for meaningless sex.'

A fleeting expression crossed his face, too quickly for her to read. 'But you made an exception for me. Am I supposed to be flattered?'

She held her head high, and said very clearly, 'If I'm pregnant, I'll take you for every cent of maintenance I can get.'

His eyes hardened. But all he said was, 'You're welcome, darling.' Then his eyes went back to the book in his hands.

Infuriated, she demanded, 'Do you always take it so lightly?'

He looked at her, his brows raised. 'What?'

Sarcastically, she said, 'I suppose you're accustomed to casual affairs with women who are always prepared. It must be terribly convenient for you.'

He put down the book and stood up, his movements very deliberate. Eloise quelled a desire to run.

He came towards her, not taking his eyes from her face. 'Actually, I'm not accustomed to casual affairs at all. I thought I'd made that clear last night—or is that another thing you "don't remember"?'

Rushing into speech, partly from sheer nervousness and partly from a desire to get at him, she said, 'I can hardly be expected to believe that! I'm sure you have Hollywood starlets falling over themselves to get into the great director's bed. And why should you resist?'

He stopped in front of her, his thumbs hooked into his belt, and rocked slightly on his heels. He looked angry and fed up, and very slightly contemptuous. 'Can't you guess?' he said grimly. 'For the very good reason that I happen to be a married man.'

CHAPTER THREE

ELOISE began to laugh.

'*Stop it!*' Angrily Greg reached for her, but she twisted away.

'You swine!' she snapped. 'Has anyone nominated you for male chauvinist of the year? It must be so handy to be able to say you're married when some poor little girl gets too clinging!'

He went quite white. 'Will you stop harping on my supposed sexual exploits? There haven't been any "poor little girls"! Not, I might add, for want of opportunity——'

'Oh, I believe *that!*'

He looked at her strangely. 'You're so bitter and twisted you won't listen to me at all, will you?' he said. 'What happened to you, Eloise? How did you get like this?'

Hurt made her voice hard, her eyes staring unblinkingly into his. 'I'll give you three guesses.'

For a long moment he stared back at her. Then he said quietly, 'What's the use?' And he spun on his heel and went straight to the door, opening and closing it without looking back. Seconds later she heard the car start and drive off down the street.

He didn't come back, and Eloise told herself she was glad, relieved, there was no future for them.

It wasn't possible to avoid all knowledge of him. Name film-makers were still a rare breed in New Zealand, and anyone in that glamorous profession who had scored even a modest success overseas was news. She switched on the television the following weekend to find him being interviewed, and watched, fascinated in spite of herself by his dark, strong face, his easy manner, his direct, intelligent answers lit with an occasional flash of self-deprecating humour.

'And what are your future plans?' the interviewer asked, after a brief discussion of the latest film which the interviewer had suggested might challenge some box office records in the United States.

The camera homed in on Greg's face, and for a moment Eloise had the strange feeling that he was looking directly at her. He hesitated.

'That depends,' he said, 'on a number of factors.'

'Professional or personal?' the interviewer questioned swiftly.

For the first time his eyes went cold, as though the question was an intrusion that he resented. Then he smiled and shrugged. 'I've learned a lot in America but I owe something to the industry in New Zealand, where I got my start. Some time I'd like to start repaying my debt.'

'So you may be staying for a while?'

Again his eyes were directly on camera, and Eloise found herself looking into them, leaning forward, waiting for his reply. 'Maybe,' he said.

The weekend newspaper carried a full-page interview too, headed 'NZ FILM INDUSTRY MAY BENEFIT FROM EXPERTISE'. She didn't read it, but she couldn't help seeing the photograph of him in evening clothes, escorting a minor film star to some Hollywood party.

Her publisher phoned her unexpectedly one day and

said, 'I have a proposition for you. Can you meet me tomorrow for lunch?'

Leon Hatfield had never offered her a publisher's lunch before. Although her books had been well reviewed, she didn't earn enough income from her two novels to live on, but her job as a librarian allowed her one afternoon off each week. 'Yes, if we can make it one o'clock,' she said.

Meeting her in the restaurant foyer, Leon said, 'Have a drink while we wait for the others.'

'What others?' she started to ask, but he was steering her to a chair, beckoning a wine waiter over. 'What would you like?'

'Oh, sherry—dry.'

When he had given the order and taken a chair beside her, she asked, 'Who else is coming?'

'A couple of film people; they want to talk to us.'

'*Film* people?'

'That's right. Now don't get your hopes up too high. Authors are apt to get dollar signs in their eyes when films are mentioned, but this is only a preliminary meeting. Even if they do ask us for an option, there's no guarantee that they'll ever pick it up.'

'I haven't got dollar signs in my eyes,' she said, 'but who are ...'

The waiter arrived with their drinks, and she fell silent while Leon paid him, leaving a tip on the tray. As the waiter departed he muttered, 'In the good old days nobody expected to be tipped in this country.' His eyes strayed past her. 'Here they are!' he said, standing up.

She followed his gaze with a sense of fatalism. At least she had been given some warning. When she looked up into a pair of appraising blue eyes and heard Leon say, 'I believe you've already met Greg Stone,' she was able to nod coolly and say, 'Yes,' and turn to his companion.

Eloise had never met a woman who fitted quite so well the description of 'willowy'. A fitted dress of some dark synthetic material showed off a figure of extreme slimness and a wonderful warm olive complexion. Sleek black hair was drawn back from a face of striking distinction, with large brown eyes and an aquiline nose set in a perfect oval.

'And this is Zuleika Osborne.'

The exotic name suited her, Eloise decided, as she returned the woman's smile.

Zuleika was a film producer. 'We've read *No Winners*,' she told Eloise, when the party was seated, 'and we think it would make a wonderful film. We'd like to buy the rights.'

Leon looked surprised and then gratified. 'I'd expected you to be asking for an option first.'

'Well, yes, but as soon as we have that, we'll be looking for finance to buy the rights. Greg will be the director, and with his name on the credits, we should be able to get the financial backing we need.'

'Well, Eloise?' Leon looked at her.

'I've never thought of it being filmed . . .' She glanced at Greg, but he was toying with his wine glass, sitting back in his chair as though withdrawing himself from the discussion.

Throughout the meal he let Zuleika do most of the talking, occasionally giving her an amiable acquiescence when she appealed to him on some point. His attitude of near boredom nettled Eloise. She kept looking at him covertly, but he seemed to be watching Zuleika, and once or twice a tolerant half-smile appeared on his lips as the producer talked, emphasising points with her long, slender hands, the fingers adorned with several large rings, her eyes flashing with excitement.

'The period feel of the book is wonderful,' she said to Eloise, who couldn't help but be flattered by the other woman's enthusiasm. 'The 1914-18 years are great for costume, too. We can dress the heroine in some of those lovely floating lacy dresses they used to wear—and big hats! Oh, she must wear a wide-brimmed picture hat for some of her scenes. Don't you think so, Greg?'

'A bit of a cliché, isn't it? I don't know how many times that scene's been done—a couple walking by a river in sunlight, with the woman wearing one of those cartwheel hats, and then cut to the same scene, and she's taken it off and is swinging it by the ribbons ...'

'They did wear them, and you'll find a way to avoid clichés, Greg.' Turning back to Eloise, Zuleika enquired, 'What made you pick that period?'

'I suppose I've always been interested in that era. My grandfather fought in the First World War, and won a medal for bravery. He would never talk about it, but my grandmother did sometimes, before she died. And— it was such a time of change and stress. The whole world altered then—from the Edwardian elegance and Victorian social mores, to the twenties, the beginning of a new world, a totally new lifestyle, but with a sort of edge of desperation and alienation.'

'One of the reviewers said there was a powerful symbolism at work,' Leon said solemnly, 'between the distance and destructiveness of the war, and the increasing distance between the two characters—the physical separation and the emotional gap that kept widening between them, as their relationship disintegrated into hatred and violence.'

Slightly embarrassed, Eloise said, 'I don't write in symbols.'

'Oh, but he's right!' Zuleika exclaimed. 'It is there, that's why the book is so powerful.'

'Then it must have been my subconscious at work. I know it felt right, that's all.' She smiled. 'You're beginning to make me uneasy! I'm wondering what else is in the book that I've missed.'

Zuleika said, laughing, 'Whatever you've put into it, it's a darned good book. I'm only sorry I haven't read it before. I do remember seeing reviews and thinking some time I'd get hold of a copy, but I never got round to it until now. Tell me though, Eloise—it's been teasing at me, and now I've got the author here, I can get the answer from the horse's mouth, so to speak—*did* the wife commit adultery? Or not?'

For a moment, Eloise felt Greg's eyes on her, but when she involuntarily shifted her gaze to meet them, he had looked away. She said, 'I don't know.'

Zuleika laughed a little incredulously. 'You don't know?'

Eloise shook her head. 'I honestly don't know. Her husband was convinced that she had. That's the vital element in the story.'

'Yes, but you never make it clear whether or not he was right.'

'It didn't seem to matter. At that point in the writing, I could only see things through his eyes. So I'm sorry, but I can't tell you. It isn't clear to me, either. Will you want to change it in the film?'

'It depends a lot on the scriptwriter and the director. Greg?'

Greg said, not looking at Eloise, 'I don't see any reason to change a good story. Actually, when I read it, my sympathy was with the husband. She could have put him out of his misery, if she was innocent.'

'Oh, you're a man, you'd take his side,' Zuleika laughed. 'Did you think she was innocent, when you read it?'

'Yes,' Greg said after a short pause. Eloise wasn't looking at him. 'I think she was.'

'Well, should we let him loose on your book, do you think, Eloise?'

'I don't know what to think,' Eloise said. 'If you don't mind my saying so, I've seen some pretty dreadful adaptations of books on film.'

Zuleika rolled her magnificent eyes. 'Haven't we all! A film can't always follow a book absolutely faithfully—it's a totally different medium. But we don't want to mutilate the book, I can assure you of that. If you like, you can have a go at writing the script yourself.'

'I have no experience with scripts.'

'Well, there's nothing to stop you trying, only we can't promise to use it. And if we do, it may be altered by the script editor or the director. Filming is always a team effort, not like writing a book. You'd be paid, though, for the time you spent on it.'

'Why don't you give it a go?' asked Leon.

'I'm not sure if I could.' They were going rather too fast for her. Leon had seemed to suggest this was a tentative meeting, and here they were talking as though the film was a *fait accompli*.

For the first time, Greg spoke directly to Eloise. 'Do you want someone else writing a script for your book?'

'They might do a better job.'

'You don't really think that.'

'You're a mind-reader?' she asked him sweetly. 'There's no end to your talents, is there?'

There was a small silence as Leon and Zuleika cast surprised looks at her, and Greg said, holding her eyes,

'You should know.'

Good manners prevented her from making a stinging rejoinder. The other two began talking to each other, discussing terms now, and Greg dropped his eyes to her clenched hands, then looked up and his lips soundlessly formed the word, 'Coward.'

Zuleika turned to her again. 'We'll probably do a lot of the filming on location. The town where your characters live—Greg thought your description fitted Thames, but you gave it a fictitious name.'

Eloise threw Greg a quick glance. He looked utterly bland. 'It was any small New Zealand town with a gold-mining history, I suppose, but I know Thames well, I was brought up near there on my parents' farm. So it was natural to use the area as a background for the novel.'

'Are they still living there?' asked Greg.

Surprised, she hesitated. 'Yes. Dad's talking of retiring soon, and going to live in town, but they're still on the farm.'

Greg nodded. 'We should take a look at the area,' he told Zuleika.

'Yes, it might be a good place to film. A couple of hours from Auckland, and there are beaches there too, up the Coromandel Peninsula from the town. Couldn't we use them for some of the scenes, Greg?'

'Still looking for cliché shots?' Greg teased, raising a brow at her.

'I'm not doing that!' Zuleika denied. 'Only they say, don't they, if you've got it, flaunt it. Well, we've got the scenery here in New Zealand to wow the movie-going public, and I think we should flaunt it for all it's worth. It's one of our greatest assets. Look what the Aussies have done with their desert reds and ochres. Our bush and our beaches have at least as much potential.'

'OK, OK, I agree with you,' Greg assured her. 'Only at times the scenery has been overworked at the expense of the story. The movie-going public may like our scenery just fine, but they come to see a story, and that's something we can't afford to forget. As for bush and beaches, sure they're beautiful and make great shots, but I seem to remember that Thames has some really interesting pioneer buildings, too. Maybe we could use some of those as well—even the workings from the old gold-mines.'

No wonder he was good, Eloise thought. He was one of the innovators whose work would always be a cut above the rest because he was able to use an original angle, find a new way of telling an old story.

After lunch, she somehow ended up being taken home by him. She had tried to refuse, but Leon had already accepted on her behalf, to her considerable annoyance, and Zuleika, who she had assumed would be with them, had gone off in a rakish sports car of her own.

'You don't really want to do this film, do you?' she asked him.

'Wrong,' he said decisively. 'I liked your book, and I want to do it very much. As a matter of fact, it was I who showed it to Zuleika.'

Surprise held her silent for a while, then she asked blankly, 'Why?'

'I told you, I liked it. I've been looking for a project interesting enough to keep me in this country—at least for a while. I bought a copy of your book because I was curious, after seeing it in your flat. It seemed to me it had great potential for film. There are some visually arresting scenes in there, plus a powerful story and a background of action. Zuleika agrees with me.'

Changing the subject, she said, 'Why do you want to stay in New Zealand? I should have thought there's a lot more for you overseas.'

'I have some unfinished business here,' he said. 'And don't tell me you don't know what it is.'

She glanced at him swiftly, then looked away. 'Whatever you do, it's nothing to do with me. Unless— you're planning to get a divorce.'

She felt his gaze on her, but it was only for a second. He had to concentrate on his driving. 'Would that interest you?' he asked her.

Her heartbeat felt suddenly slow and heavy. She tightened her grip on the bag in her lap and said, 'I don't really care, one way or the other.'

He changed gear to round a corner, then said, 'I take it that you're not pregnant?'

'No,' she said, steadying her voice with some effort. 'I'm not.'

'Disappointed?'

She turned to stare at him. 'Certainly not!'

He looked at her for a moment with an unreadable expression. 'I am.'

Eloise drew a deep, uneven breath. 'What on earth do you mean?'

'What I said. I'd like to have fathered a child by you.'

For a moment she was speechless. She had a strong desire to yell and throw something. Fortunately the interior of the car was lacking in lethal objects. She managed to limit herself to saying acidly, 'In the circumstances, that's not only ridiculous, it's downright disgusting!'

She saw his mouth tighten, though he didn't look at her again. 'Find another word, Eloise.'

'Why? So that *you* can feel better about what

hap——' *no*, her mind said, and she clamped her teeth firmly in front of her tongue.

'If you mean the other night, I feel pretty good about what happened, as a matter of fact.'

She had to stop the retort which rose automatically to her lips. Instead she said tightly, 'I'm glad somebody feels good about it, because *I* don't. I feel dirty and—degraded.'

Unusually for him, he grated the gears as he changed up. Suddenly savage, he said, 'You have no sense of self-preservation, do you?'

They were nearly there. He drove tight-lipped the rest of the way, and stopped outside her flat.

'Thank you for the lift,' she said with chilly politeness.

'Ask me in.'

'You must be crazy! After the last time . . .?'

'*Last time*, sweetheart,' he said between his teeth, 'you *liked* it—at least as much as I did.'

'I told you——'

'Oh, sure, you were tipsy, didn't know what you were doing, weren't responsible . . . You had two glasses of wine at lunch, is that going to make you paralytic? Or turn you into a nymphomaniac?'

'Why do you want to come in? We've nothing to talk abou——'

'The film. Let's discuss the film, shall we?'

'There's no need to be sarcastic!'

He seemed to take a pull on himself. 'I wasn't intending to be. I always work closely with the writer if I can, and especially where we're dealing with an adaptation.'

She looked at him uncertainly. 'Do you really want to film my book, or is it . . .'

'An excuse?' His smile was impatient. 'Think about

it, Eloise. I could have dreamed up a hundred less expensive excuses to see you.'

She hadn't been thinking in terms of excuses, rather of something more sinister. She shook her head. 'That wasn't what I meant.'

'What did you mean?'

'It doesn't matter.' She paused. 'Come in, then, if you really have something to say.'

Greg refused coffee, and didn't seem to want to sit down. He shoved his hands into his pockets and prowled restlessly as he talked. 'It's natural for a writer to be nervous, especially in the light of what's been done to some good books in the past. But you have the chance to do the script yourself, and as I said, I like to work with the writer. I'm not a subscriber to the *auteur*-director theory. As Zuleika said today, filming is teamwork, and unless a director writes the script himself, it seems to me somewhat arrogant to claim all the credit.'

'Would I be able to sit in on the filming?'

'I hope you will. The writer is the one who knows the characters from the inside out, if anyone does, and I know that it's often a help to the actors, too, being able to go to the person who invented their character and say, "Hey, how does this guy tick? What am I supposed to be portraying here?"'

'And you don't mind that?'

'No, I like to be a part of those discussions too. You'll find it different from working alone with your type-writer. But stimulating. Have you seen any of my films?'

'Not those you've made in America. I don't go to films much.'

She wasn't looking at him, and he regarded her downbent head thoughtfully for a moment. 'I've worked with some really good people,' he said. 'And Zuleika and

I have already talked about who we'd like for this one. Stars, camera operators, the costume designer. All Kiwis. It's a New Zealand story and we want to do it with our own people, not imports. We think the world is ready for us.'

'My book isn't a best-seller in New Zealand, and it hasn't even been published overseas. No one will have heard of it.'

'Doesn't matter. Lots of great films have been made from almost unknown books. A film should boost the sales, though. There hasn't been much done about New Zealand at war. The Australians are well ahead of us in that department. Let's do it, Eloise. Doesn't it excite you?'

Greg's controlled enthusiasm did excite her, but she tried to put a brake on her feelings. 'I don't know if I have the time to write a script. I have a job, and I'm working on another book.'

Greg sat down on the sofa opposite her. 'Wouldn't you like the chance to write full time? You'd probably get enough money for the option to take two or three months off and write the script. And enough from the script, even if they don't use it, to keep yourself while you finish your next novel. Think about it.'

He must have seen that she was tempted. He stood up again and walked to the window, turning with his hands in his pockets. 'You've written a good story. I think you could turn it into a good script. The thing to remember is that film is a totally visual medium.' He paused again, staring at her, then seemed to collect himself. 'Think in terms of pictures—a series of pictures you're presenting to the audience.'

'Quite a lot of the book is what happens in the characters' minds,' Eloise reminded him.

'Some of that can be expressed in their actions, in the settings, even the music. Don't think only in terms of dialogue.'

He was talking quite fast, his manner impersonal, but she had the impression his mind was not entirely on what he was saying. His next remark confirmed it. 'How long did it take to get the book published?' he asked.

'About a year from when it was accepted. A bit more. Why?'

He cast her an odd look. 'It will be at least that long before the film is finished, too. How long did it take you to write it?'

'About ten, eleven months.'

'And was Leon's firm the first publisher you submitted it to?'

'No, the third. What does this have to do with ...'

'Making a film script of it?' He shrugged. 'I was just curious. You must have started writing it years ago.' When she didn't answer, he switched the subject again. 'I can give you a list of some of the best scripts if you like. The library should have some in book form and—do you have a video player?' He looked about the room.

'No, but I suppose I could hire one.'

'There are some good films on tape. Why don't you come round and watch some of my classics, and I'll show you what I mean?'

She hesitated, and he said drily, 'That's not the latest version of "Come and see my etchings". It's a genuine offer.'

She flushed. 'I know that. You're being—very kind.'

Greg's mouth thinned perceptibly. 'Do me a favour, Eloise,' he said. 'Don't treat me like a stranger.'

She looked down at her hands. 'I feel—that's what you are.'

He said harshly, 'How can you say that?' He had left the window, halting half-way across the room.

'You said we'd talk about the film,' she reminded him.

'Yes.' He wheeled, going back to the window. 'This is a very sensitive story,' he said. 'You've captured the theme of the disintegrating marriage after an idyllic start very well.' His head turned, his gaze on her sharp, probing.

'It's hardly a new theme.'

'There are no new themes. Only new ways to express them.' He came towards her again. 'I find it interesting that you've told the story mainly from the man's angle.'

Her swift gaze stopped him in his tracks. 'It's fiction,' she said.

His mouth twisted. 'I wondered why you chose to do it that way.'

She shrugged. 'It's more of a challenge.'

There was a heartbeat's silence. She wasn't looking at him any more, but she could feel his eyes on her. Slowly, he said, 'They say that first novels are often largely autobiographical.'

She looked up, her face hostile, defensive. 'This one wasn't!'

'Are you sure? I don't think authors always realise how much of themselves they unwittingly reveal in their books.'

Eloise sat very still. 'As I said at lunch, people tend to read a great deal into some books that isn't really there.'

Greg said, 'I'm sure you would admit there are parallels.'

'They're very general ones. You just said there are no new themes. Every book must reflect someone's life.'

'And some reflections are more true to life than others.'

'Are we discussing art?' Eloise asked, her voice brittle. 'Or life?'

'We're not discussing anything,' he replied with a hint of sarcasm. 'I'm trying to discuss ... but you're fencing.'

Standing up, she said, 'If we've finished talking about the possibility of a film, perhaps you'd like to go.'

He was looking at her with an expression of angry frustration, his eyes narrow and his mouth tight. 'You can't run away from it for ever,' he told her. 'Be as stubborn as you like, but one day you'll back yourself into a corner, and there'll be no way out.'

CHAPTER FOUR

ELOISE returned Aaron's shirt, and almost reluctantly asked for his advice on scriptwriting. He had written for television and scripted several New Zealand films. When she told him why she was asking, he was delighted, and lent her some books that he had found useful himself. Fascinated in spite of herself, she began to go through them, and was caught up in the theories and practical difficulties of a new craft. When she switched on the television she couldn't help analysing with a much more informed eye what she saw, even thinking occasionally that she could do better herself. When Leon phoned again she said, 'Let them have the rights. I want to do the script.'

Acting on Aaron's advice, she had decided to do a scene breakdown first, dividing the story into scenes, then add the dialogue and specific actions, and worry about the rather daunting special requirements for script layout afterwards, when she came to the final copy.

Re-reading the book, Greg's remarks about autobiographical first novels and writers revealing themselves kept coming to mind, and she saw parallels with her own life which had not consciously occurred to her when she wrote the story. The historical background and the feeling of writing about other people in a different time had disguised them, but now she saw uneasily that perhaps her subconscious had drawn more heavily than she had realised on experience to create the novel which she had thought was totally invented. Although only the odd incident or two could be called loosely based on actual events, now she wondered if she had after all begun writing it as some kind of purge of her own emotions. Sometimes she was embarrassed by a passage which seemed to reflect all too clearly her own feelings in similar circumstances.

Greg phoned and said, 'Zuleika tells me we have an option. She's getting the wheels in motion to get finance and pick up the rights. I believe you're doing the script. How about those videos?'

'Yes. When can I see them?'

'Tonight, if you like. I'll give you dinner first.'

'That isn't necessary.'

'Eloise, let's try to establish an atmosphere of friendly co-operation, OK? Shall I pick you up?'

'No, I'll get there on my own. Tell me where.'

He was living in a rented house, a comfortable, well preserved old home with high ceilings and big rooms. There was a formal dining-room, with two places laid, linen table mats on pale polished wood.

'Shrimps in avocado, followed by a chicken salad and cheese,' he said.

'It sounds fine.' Eloise had always loved seafoods and had never been particularly fond of red meat or sweets, eating them only rarely. She sipped at the white wine he had poured into her glass.

When she had drained her second glass of wine, having finished eating, he made to refill it, but she put her hand over the glass, shaking her head.

'Cheese?'

She helped herself to some cheese and a biscuit, and looked up to find him watching her over his glass.

Involuntarily, she said, 'I wish you wouldn't do that.'

'Do what?'

'Look at me like that.'

'Like what?' He put his glass down as though he was really interested in her answer.

She looked back at him with exasperation. 'As though I'm a puzzle that you're trying to solve. It's—unnerving.'

'Why?' His eyes were very blue and penetrating. 'Have you got a guilty conscience?' he asked softly.

Eloise pushed her plate away.

'You haven't eaten your cheese,' he pointed out.

'I'm not hungry any more—thank you.'

'You don't have to be polite with me, Eloise.'

'I'll take the dishes to the kitchen while you finish your wine.' She stacked the dishes with hands that were not quite steady.

Greg came to the kitchen too and stood in the doorway behind her. 'Don't bother washing them,' he said. 'I'll do them in the morning.'

'All right.' She turned just as he stepped forward to put his glass on the sink bench, and they almost collided. His fingers fell on her shoulder, and gripped. The glass clattered on to the bench and rolled noisily into the sink. His face was very close, his mouth inches from hers. Her eyes widened and he said, 'Well . . .'

Eloise moved, pulling away, and backed against the bench, holding its edge. His hand left her shoulder and dropped to his side. He was still very close. He said again, on a different inflection, 'Well?'

She shook her head.

Greg laughed, a little harshly. 'How long do you think you can hold out? Your reactions are unexpected, I admit—but unmistakable.'

She didn't bother to deny it. 'There's more to life than sex.'

'And you an aspiring scriptwriter! Try to find some more original lines than that, won't you?'

'Yes.' It was all she could manage. 'I will.' His sarcasm was withering, but preferable to that dangerous proximity.

'You can let go of the bench now. I'm not going to leap on you. Come on, we'd better watch some videos. It's what you came for.'

She sat in an armchair facing the TV screen, and Greg sprawled on the floor on a pile of cushions, with the remote control in his hand, occasionally fast-forwarding or going back to review a piece of film that he wanted her specially to take note of. Sometimes Eloise thought he had forgotten her presence, his eyes intent on the film, his face thoughtful, but then he would say, 'Watch this bit carefully, see how the cut between scenes picks up on the dialogue.' Or, 'Did you notice how that was done? There's no dialogue needed. It's all shown to the viewer.'

And once, when a long, explicit love scene was playing, he glanced at her, while she kept her eyes resolutely glued to the screen.

At midnight he switched off. 'Enough for one evening, I think.'

She said, 'Yes. Thank you for the dinner, and the videos.'

'I'll make some coffee and run you home.'

'There's no need. Just call me a cab, please.'

'Don't argue. Why haven't you got yourself a car?'

It was a question she had fielded before. The answer came out carelessly pat. 'I can't be bothered with the hassles—parking, petrol, repairs. I find buses and taxis quite adequate and possibly not as expensive in the long run.'

Greg accepted the explanation without comment. 'Coffee coming up.'

When he came back carrying two steaming cups, she

saw that he had already added cream to hers.

'No mints, I'm afraid,' he said.

'It's all right.'

'That's right, you don't eat them, do you?'

She didn't answer, bending her head to sip at her coffee. He lounged at her feet, leaning against the arm of the chair.

'This is cosy,' he said. 'Brings back memories.'

She still didn't answer, and he turned to look up at her. 'Your cue,' he told her, 'to say, "What memories?" Or can you guess?'

Eloise put down her half-finished coffee and stood up. 'I'll call my own cab,' she said.

But he had stood up, too, leaving his cup on the floor by the chair. He blocked her way, put a hand on her arm, looking at her averted head. 'You don't have to be scared of me. Let *go*, darling, let go.'

The tenderness in his voice was almost her undoing. She swayed slightly towards him, heard him draw in a quick breath, and abruptly steadied herself. His other hand grasped her shoulder, and when she tried to step back it tightened.

Her head went up and her eyes met his. 'Why?' she demanded. 'So that I can have my heart trampled on all over again—just to satisfy your masculine pride, to prove to yourself that you're irresistible?'

'That isn't fair!' He tried to bring her closer, but she pulled away strongly and swept his hands aside.

'Memories!' she said scornfully. 'Yes, I could swap memories with you. Memories of a man who promised me happiness, who said he loved me, and would cherish me all my life, a man I was certain would never hurt me, never doubt me—who would always be there when I needed him . . .'

'Eloise . . .'

'And I have other memories . . .' *Memories of pain and fear and darkness, memories of calling his name when I was alone and needing him—needing him desperately to be with me—and he wasn't there. He never came.*

She blinked away tears, clenched her teeth and said, 'Leave me alone, can't you? Why do you want to rake over things I'd rather forget? What kind of sadist are you?' Her eyes were diamond-bright, her cheeks hot. 'Go and play your nasty little games with someone else!'

'Eloise . . .' He looked pale now, his mouth grim, a frown between the dark, straight brows. His voice was unsteady. 'Eloise—I'm sorry.'

'Yes,' she said shakily, 'I'm sure you are. You didn't mean to stir that up, did you?'

'If I say no, that doesn't mean——'

'You wanted me to remember the nice things, didn't you—sickly, sentimental things—kisses and the wine——? Oh, I remember them, all right. Making love in a field of dog-daisies, and having dinner by candlelight in a new flat with no furniture except one armchair and the bed, and dancing all night in a waterfront café and walking along the beach barefoot at dawn. I remember all that—staying in bed all day on a rainy Saturday listening to the radio and eating peanuts, going to our first cricket match and neither of us knowing who was out and who was in, and attending some dreadful play and writing our own rude review of it afterwards. I remember those, too. But unfortunately it doesn't cancel out the other.' She shook her head fiercely, fighting back tears, her teeth clenched. 'It doesn't!'

'I didn't suppose it could,' he said quietly. 'But give me a chance, Eloise—a chance to make new memories for you, a whole lot of new ones, good ones, and in time, they'll outweigh the others . . .'

'Is that what you want?' Blank surprise showed in her face. 'Is that what you really want?'

'What did you think?' he said, frowning. 'You were the one who talked about one-night stands and meaningless sex. I want much more than that. You're not the only one who's been hurt and disappointed. The last few years haven't been all a bed of roses for me, either. But it's no use living in the past. The future is what matters—for both of us.' His eyes didn't waver from her face. His voice was quiet, but intense, deep. '*I promise I'll make it come right for you, Eloise.*'

'Someone else might,' she said cruelly. 'But not you, Greg. You're the last man to be able to do that for me.'

'Perhaps,' he said slowly, 'I'm the only man who can.'

She looked at him with derision. 'And just how do you work that out?'

'There must have been other candidates. And none of them measure up?'

'I wasn't measuring.'

'I'll bet you were,' he argued, anger flickering in his eyes. 'Comparing them all with this mythical dream man who lives in your head, and they all fell short. Just as I did. Why don't you grow up, Eloise? The perfect man doesn't exist. We all have faults—we all make mistakes—sometimes enormous ones. I'm sorry—desperately sorry, that you were so hurt, but can't you see how much more you're hurting yourself? All that bitterness you're feeding inside you, it's twisting your emotions, drying up your soul!'

'When I need psychoanalysis,' she said coldly, 'I'll go to a professional, thank you. Have you quite finished?'

She made to turn away, but his hand closed round her arm, forcefully.

'What do I have to do to make you *listen?*' he said. Then his tone changed, his expression became analytical, almost cold. 'I've read your second book, you know. It's not as good as the first. And do you know why? Because you've lost some of the feeling, the involvement with the characters that carried the first one. Oh, the writing is first-rate and the dialogue sparkles, your technique has even improved. But there's something missing. There's no heart in it. And I'd bet the next one is even more slick and technically brilliant—and empty at the core.'

She jerked her arm free of his hold and stepped away from him. 'Well, now that you've picked apart both my character and my writing,' she said, 'perhaps you'll allow me to go home.'

His eyes suddenly blazed. 'There's only one way to get through to you, isn't there?'

Eloise went taut and still, and he laughed shortly. 'Oh, don't worry. It doesn't last, you'd be retreating from reality twice as fast again in the morning, I know that. And doing your damnedest to punish me for breaking through the barriers, even temporarily. Come on, before the temptation gets too much for me—I'll take you home.'

CHAPTER FIVE

ELOISE gave in her notice at the library, and began to concentrate in earnest on the script for the film. She had signed the contract giving the film company an option, and Zuleika had arranged an advance on payment for the script, so that she would be able to survive while she worked on it full time.

For the moment her next novel had been shelved, and she tried to push out of her mind Greg's caustic opinion of its possibilities. She had written a number of short stories as well as the novels, some of which had been published in literary magazines, and one had been picked up for an anthology. No one else had suggested that her style was slick but shallow.

Aaron phoned. 'I hear you're a full-time scriptwriter now. How's it going?'

'Slowly,' she said. 'I seem to be stuck after scene twenty-two. There's nothing really visual in the book at that point, but I can't skip the next chapter because it's all about motivation, and I feel that's terribly important.'

'You're right,' he said. 'It is. Why not have lunch with me tomorrow, and I'll help out if I can.'

'I'd be grateful.' Greg had told her to contact him if she had any problems, but she was reluctant to do that.

It was a leisurely lunch, and over coffee afterwards, which they took on a terrace with a view of the Waitemata Harbour, Eloise drew out a few typewritten pages and a copy of her book from a slim satchel, and said, 'Look, this is where I've got to. If you have any suggestions . . .'

Aaron moved his chair round, laying his arm along the back of hers, and they pored over the pages together. Half an hour later, she sat back and smiled at him. 'That's it, of course. I don't know why I couldn't see it for myself. Thanks so much, Aaron.'

He turned his head and dropped a quick, warm kiss on her lips. Lifting his head, he said quizzically, 'Do you mind?'

She shook her head, but moved a little away. 'In the circumstances you deserve it. But don't let it become a habit.'

'It could be a very nice habit,' he sighed. 'Are you an ice maiden with everyone?'

Eloise picked up her satchel and began putting away the typescript. 'Don't worry, it isn't something your best friend wouldn't tell you about.' As she lifted her head, her glance collided with a blue, accusing one and she straightened abruptly.

Greg had stopped in the doorway of the terrace, his hand on Zuleika Osborne's arm, but his gaze on Eloise.

'Talk of the devil,' said Aaron softly.

Wrenching her eyes back to him, she said, 'Were we?'

'No, but I was thinking of Greg Stone, and there he is,' Aaron murmured. 'Actually I wanted to ask you about . . .'

'What?' Resolutely she fixed her attention on him.

But he had looked past her and was rising to his feet. Greg's voice said, 'Hello, Aaron—Eloise.'

Eloise put a smile on her face and directed it somewhere in the region of Greg's top shirt button, which was undone, as was the next one. Well, it was a warm day. Only she wished that he didn't look so—there was only one word for it—sexy. Aaron had actually left even more buttons open, exposing a beautifully tanned chest adorned with a silver medallion, but the sight of it hadn't increased her heartbeat by one flutter, hadn't made her blood suddenly roar through her veins ...

Zuleika said, 'What a nice surprise to find you here, Eloise,' and with relief she dragged her attention to the other woman. 'We were just discussing you, as a matter of fact,' Zuleika told her, 'or rather, your book.' She paused, turning an enquiring glance on Aaron.

Eloise introduced them. 'Zuleika's the producer of the film,' she explained.

Aaron shook hands with Zuleika, leaning forward so that he almost teetered on his feet, eyes gazing earnestly into hers, seemingly in two minds whether to kneel and kiss one of her several rings. He pulled out a chair for her, practically inviting her to wipe her feet on him. 'Please—join us, do sit down. Delighted to meet you. Have you ordered? Let me get you a coffee—Eloise, another cup?'

Zuleika sat down gracefully. Greg, who looked as though he would have preferred to refuse, followed suit, seating himself between Zuleika and Eloise, and Aaron fussed over their orders and hailed a waiter in a loud voice to fulfil them.

Zuleika said to Eloise, 'How is the script coming along?'

'It's going to be a great script,' said Aaron. 'This girl has loads of talent.'

Zuleika smiled, and Greg said rather sharply, 'You've seen it?'

'Just been going over it,' Aaron confirmed. 'You'll love it.'

'Well, perhaps you'd let me see it, some time,' drawled Greg, his eyes like ice chips as they rested on Eloise.

'Yes, of course,' she said equally coolly, 'only I'd like to have it a bit more finished first.'

'Don't go too far,' he said. 'If you're haring off in all the wrong directions, it could be a lot of work wasted, unless you take some advice early on.'

'I just did,' she replied, 'from Aaron. He's a very experienced scriptwriter.'

'Oh, that's where I've heard your name!' Zuleika said to Aaron. 'Of course, you did the script for *Sunshine Season*, didn't you?'

'That's right,' Aaron admitted, trying to look modest. 'And a few others.'

'Tell me!' she commanded.

Aaron told her, losing with remarkably good grace his battle for modesty.

'You are experienced,' said Zuleika. 'That's quite an impressive list of credits.'

Aaron shrugged. 'I'm glad you think so. Actually——' He paused. 'Well, as a matter of fact, I was going to ask Eloise if she'd mind putting in a word for me.'

'About——?'

'If you need a script editor on this film, I'd like to apply for the job.'

'We don't need one,' Greg said positively.

Zuleika cast him a surprised look. 'I don't remember discussing it.'

'We haven't.'

'Maybe we should give it some thought. I know that Eloise was a bit nervous about doing it on her own——'

'You said yourself,' Eloise reminded him, 'that filming is teamwork. I've found Aaron's help invaluable.'

Greg said, 'I've already told you to call on me if you need advice. Script editors cost money, and we'll be working on a tight budget.'

'I don't know, though,' said Zuleika, as the waiter
arrived with a tray. 'It might be a very good idea to put a
competent script editor on the film. Of course, you'd
have the final say, Greg. But if Eloise feels it would be
helpful, I think the budget can stand it.'

'I'd like to work with Aaron,' Eloise said firmly. 'He
has a knack of putting his finger on what's wrong, and
he doesn't try to impose his own ideas on me.'

Greg gave her a hard look, and she returned it with
one of defiance.

Zuleika said, 'We'll talk it over and let you know,
Aaron.' She handed the sugar to Greg, who shook his
head. Aaron squeezed Eloise's hand under cover of the
table and whispered, 'Thanks, doll!'

She gave him a little smile. Greg was scowling at her
across the table, and although she told herself he had
neither right nor reason, she couldn't help feeling
nervous and guilty.

As soon as she decently could, she excused herself,
saying she wanted to get back to work on the script now
that Aaron had helped her out of the hole she had been
in. Aaron insisted on running her home, and talked all
the way about the good luck that had led Greg and
Zuleika to the restaurant at just the right time. 'And
thanks, love, for putting your oar in. I won't forget it,
believe me. To get my name on the credits of a Greg
Stone film certainly isn't going to do me any harm
career-wise. You're an angel, Eloise.'

'You haven't got the job yet,' she reminded him.

His happy mood slipped a little. 'No, and if Greg has
his way, I might not. I've never been exactly close to
him, but we always got on pretty well when our paths
crossed. Why did I get the impression today that he
doesn't like me?'

'You're imagining it.'

'No, I'm not. I'm a writer, dear, a sensitive soul. I feel these things in my bones. Not that a bull mastiff wouldn't have noticed the atmosphere.' He looked at her curiously. 'I heard a little rumour the other day—about you and him. Couldn't believe it at the time, was it just one of those ridiculous stories that get around, or——?'

'You shouldn't listen to rumours, Aaron. And you certainly shouldn't believe them.'

He eyed her shrewdly. 'Well, dear, if you say so. Then you and Greg Stone aren't——' he wiggled his hand expressively.

'I've written a book that he's filming, that's all.'

He looked sceptical, but didn't press her. 'Oh, well, I can hope to have made a good impression on the lovely Zuleika, anyway. She seemed to like me all right.'

'I'm sure she did. She'd be a fool not to.'

'You're good for my ego—sometimes. Here we are. Are you going to ask me in, or are you serious about getting back to the grindstone?'

'Serious. But thanks for the lunch, and even more so for the help. I won't ask again unless you're paid for it by the film company.'

'Cross your fingers for me, darling. And if you have any influence with the stony Greg, do you think you could bring yourself to exert it on my behalf?'

'I'd probably only make matters worse.'

He looked at her thoughtfully. 'Ah! Sorry, that was silly of me.'

Exasperated, she said, 'Would you believe I don't have the slightest idea what you're talking about?'

Aaron shook his head and looked wise. 'I don't know why I didn't wake up to it before, except that you're so darned secretive. It's that gorgeous Mona Lisa face of yours, not giving a thing away.'

'Aaron!'

'Never mind, I won't tell a soul. Not a soul. Promise. Only, if I were you, I'd be careful of making that guy jealous. From all accounts, he's got a nasty temper when he's crossed.'

She knew that, Eloise thought grimly, as she let herself into the flat. But she was damned if she was going to let it bother her. Not that she had any intention of trying to make Greg jealous. She wondered if he and Zuleika had been having a business lunch, or a private one. She recalled him saying, 'I happen to be a married man.'

But not very, she thought cynically. It certainly didn't seem to cramp his style much.

She had scarcely settled back at the typewriter when the telephone bell cut into her concentration.

Glaring at it, she was tempted to let it go on ringing until whoever it was gave up. Perhaps, if she was going to keep working at home, she should think about getting an answering machine.

Eventually, she picked up the receiver. If she didn't she would only spend the rest of the day wondering who had been trying to contact her, and whether or not it was important.

'Eloise?' her mother's voice said, and Eloise felt her heart sink. 'I knew you must be home.'

'How? I didn't know you were clairvoyant.'

'Well, it's Wednesday.'

'Is it? I'd forgotten.'

'What do you mean?'

She could have bitten off her tongue. Of course, her mother didn't know yet that Wednesday wasn't the only afternoon she could be expected to be at home now. Every Wednesday for the last three years she had done a little shopping and then hurried back to the flat to write.

It had been difficult at first persuading her mother that she wasn't available for extended shopping trips in Queen Street, and that phone calls were not always a welcome interruption. 'I'm sorry, Mum,' she said hastily. 'I was thinking of something else. I'm rather busy.' She cast a longing glance at the typewriter, trying to retain in her head the last sentence which she had just half written.

'Well, I'm sorry if I'm interrupting, dear,' her mother said.

'It's all right, really.' Eloise felt a familiar pang of guilt. 'What did you want?'

'What's this about you writing a film—for Greg Stone? It isn't true, is it?'

Hedging, Eloise asked, 'Where did you hear that?'

'I was just talking to some ladies at the Women's Institute, they said it was in the paper. Well, I told them it's the first I've heard of it. But if it's in the paper . . . Eloise, what is going on?'

Eloise shut her eyes. 'I'll come down at the weekend, Mum. Let's talk about it then, shall we?'

'Then it is true? But Eloise . . .'

'Look, I'm sorry, but I really am busy. And I'm sorry you found out from someone else. I wanted to tell you myself.'

'I saw him on television, being interviewed. Did you see——'

'Yes, I did,' Eloise interrupted. 'But I don't want to discuss it right now. I'll see you on Saturday.'

At last she managed to ring off, knowing her mother was upset and a little offended. She sighed and scowled at the typewriter, willing herself back into working mode. The weekend was going to be difficult.

Her parents had never had an easy life financially and for her mother, especially, 'security' was a primary aim in life. In their terms that meant a good steady job, or a good steady husband. Their only daughter had alarmed them by her singular ambition, announcing at an early age that she wanted to be a writer. 'You can't make a living at writing stories,' they said, after conferring with teachers and careers advisors. 'It's very nice for a hobby, but what will you do for a *real* job?'

When she found a job in the public library, Eloise was satisfied to be working with books and people who appreciated them, pursuing a career which fed and clothed her and fitted in perfectly with her major ambition, and her parents breathed a heartfelt sigh of relief. Librarians in their eyes embodied the height of respectability. Eloise wondered what they would have made of some of the conversations in the staff-room, and whether they had any idea of the content of the books which certainly helped to widen her horizons in several directions. She had learned that library workers were necessarily among the most unshockable people in the world, and where the stereotype of the sexually repressed spinster librarian had come from she couldn't imagine.

On Friday night she was packing when the doorbell rang. Holding some clothes which she had just ironed, Eloise opened the door to find Greg standing there, his eyes very blue and hard. 'Ask me in,' he said.

Mutely she stood aside. He shut the door, and as he turned he seemed so close that she instinctively made a hurried movement away from him. A freshly ironed blouse fell to the floor, and he picked it up for her.

'Thank you,' she said. 'I'll just put these away.'

She expected him to wait for her in the living-room. Instead, he followed her into the bedroom, lounging in the doorway as she placed the ironed clothing carefully into the overnight bag resting on the bed.

'Going away?' he enquired.

'Yes.'

'For the weekend?'

'That's right.' She turned. 'Shall we go into the lounge?'

He looked around the room, letting his eyes rest on the bed for a moment. 'I like it here,' he said. 'It brings back pleasant memories.'

Not deigning to answer, Eloise swept past him with her head held high and her eyes fixed straight ahead.

In the other room, she said, 'Would you like a drink?'

'What do you have?'

'I don't keep a lot of alcohol, but there's some quite good whisky.'

'No, thanks. A coffee would be nice, though.'

'Sit down,' she said firmly, not wanting him crowding her in the kitchen, where she couldn't reasonably expect him to keep his distance.

When she brought the coffee, he sat back on the sofa and regarded her thoughtfully over the steaming cup. He said, 'Tell me something. Why are you so anxious to have Aaron Colfax edit your script?'

'I'm not anxious,' she protested. 'Only he seems good, I know I can work with him, and he's very well qualified for the job, isn't he?'

'Yes, he is. I told you to contact me if you ran into any problems.'

'I probably would have, eventually, but Aaron happened to phone just at the right time, and I asked him instead. I found him easy to work with.'

'You feel you can work better with him than with me?'

She glanced at him fleetingly. 'Actually, yes.'

'Why?'

This time she held his gaze for longer. 'I'm sure you know why.'

'I'm still the director. You'll have to work with me, eventually. Are you regretting signing that contract?'

'No.' She added honestly, 'Any writer would be thrilled at the prospect of you directing the film of their book. Whatever our personal—differences—I'm still pleased and proud that you want to do it.'

He looked faintly surprised. 'Thanks. Flattery from you is somewhat—unexpected.'

'It isn't flattery. It's the truth.'

He drank some of his coffee, then with both hands holding his cup, he said, 'You'll probably get Aaron for script editor. Zuleika seems quite keen on the idea. She thinks I'm only stalling because I like to keep all the reins in my own hands.'

Eloise took a sip of the hot coffee. She looked at him cautiously. He seemed to be waiting for her to respond, but that was dangerous ground, and she decided not to comment.

'Are you expecting someone?' he asked.

'No, why?'

'You seem nervous.'

'I'm always nervous around you,' she admitted without thinking.

His eyes went hard. 'How long are you going to keep this up?'

She shook her head. 'I didn't mean—oh, never mind.'

Greg drained his cup and put it down on the table with an impatient thud. 'You said you don't have a boyfriend,' he said. 'Let me guess—you're going to visit your parents.'

Warily she drank some more coffee, avoiding his eyes. 'Yes, I am, as a matter of fact.'

'How are you getting there?'

'I have a bus ticket.'

'I'll drive you.'

She put down her own cup. 'No, thank you. I've bought the ticket.'

'You can get a refund. You'd be a lot more comfortable in my car.'

'No, I wouldn't,' she said feelingly.

His glance was sharp. 'Simply because I'd be there.'

'Exactly.' She met his eyes.

He was inspecting her with interest. 'That's something of an admission,' he said softly.

She flushed. 'That isn't what I meant!'

His eyes were fixed on her face now, and his mouth had gone straight. 'You have nothing to fear from me, and you know it,' he said.

'How could I possibly know that?' she asked bitingly. 'Simply on your say-so? Don't make me laugh!'

'The first time I came here, I thought I'd pretty well proved it. Oh, you pretended for a while that you couldn't stand the sight of me, but I'm not so dumb that I don't know when a woman wants me. I won't say I wasn't surprised—but I was not mistaken.'

'I'd had plenty of Dutch courage,' Eloise snapped back.

He suddenly laughed. 'That's rubbish and you know it. Come on, Eloise, let's call a truce. We have to work together. It won't do either us or the film any good if we keep tearing each other apart.'

He could be very persuasive. She had forgotten how his smile could alter the hard planes of his face, and bring an almost tender light to his eyes.

'I don't want to fight,' she said stiffly.

'Good. That's makes two of us.' He stood up, and tugged her to her feet. 'Friends?'

She nodded, trying unobtrusively to withdraw from

his light hold. But he drew her closer just for a second, and dropped a kiss on her lips, immediately releasing her. 'I'd really like to take you down to Thames,' he said. 'It would be a good chance to look round the area, as we're thinking of shooting there. Especially with you along. I'd find it extremely useful, and since you're going anyway——'

Somehow she had been manoeuvred, but with the truce they had agreed so new, she didn't want to disturb the delicate balance of their relationship. And she was still feeling stupidly breathless from that fleeting touch of his lips on hers.

Her parents wouldn't meet the bus unless she phoned and asked them to. She had friends who made regular trips to Thames and her mother knew that if she had been offered a lift they would probably bring her to the farm. She would get Greg to drop her in the town and then telephone for them to collect her, so that he wouldn't have to see them.

'All right,' she agreed. 'If it would help, you can drive me down.'

CHAPTER SIX

GREG picked her up quite early. Eloise had pulled on a pair of jeans and a loose knitted top, and the way he looked at her when she opened the door to him, she might as well have worn nothing at all. She found herself prickling with a mixture of annoyance and something else she didn't want to recognise. He smiled at her as though he knew all about it, and she left the door wide and said, 'I'll get my bag. I won't be long.'

'I'll carry it,' he said, and followed her into the bedroom.

She tossed in her brush and comb and a make-up bag, and zipped up the overnighter. Greg leaned past her to pick it up, and she stepped back quickly, almost losing her balance.

His arm brushed hers as he lifted the bag, and he turned his head, his eyes glinting. 'Oh, for crying out loud!' Throwing the bag on to the bed, he grabbed her shoulders, and then his mouth came down on hers.

She strained silently against him, her closed fists beating at his chest, her teeth clenched and lips tightly shut, but he kept on kissing her, eventually taking her wrists and holding them behind her, bringing her body into intimate contact with his, one hand tangled in her hair, his mouth still taking its toll, until at last it seemed he had had enough. Then he pushed her away, breathing hard, and said, 'That's what you've been expecting, isn't it—an attack? Well, you finally got it. And don't look so shattered. That's all that's going to happen, you needn't worry any more. Now let's get on, shall we?'

He swung the bag off the bed again and strode out of the room. She heard him open the outer door, and stood where he had left her.

She wouldn't go with him, she would tell him the trip was off. But she had cancelled her bus ticket and her parents were expecting her.

He was slamming the boot when she went out to the car, hardly glancing at her as he opened the passenger door. But after he had slid into the driver's seat, he sat staring straight ahead and holding the wheel with both hands until the knuckles showed white. 'I didn't mean to do that,' he said bleakly. 'I promise it won't happen again. But do you think you could stop flinching from me every time I come near you? I find it an unbearable provocation.'

'Do you blame me?' she asked bitterly, touching lips that still stung.

His mouth compressed, and she saw the swift rise of colour in his face. 'Perhaps not,' he said quietly. 'But that night after the party—you didn't shrink from me then. Far from it. Why now?'

'I'll try not to,' she told him obliquely, 'if you keep your promise.'

He looked at her then as though he wanted to say something more. But after a moment he just shrugged, and started the engine.

Before long they had left the city behind and were cresting the Bombay Hill, with its soft, panoramic views of distant, dreaming hills and green farmland. At the bottom of the long, curving slope they turned off the main road south to head towards the coast, and after a while the neatly fenced farms began to include hills covered in second-growth bush, white-flowered manuka and gracefully curved ferns. The day was hot, the sky a brilliant blue with few clouds, and as they passed another patch of bush, the song of a thousand cicadas penetrated into the car.

They talked little. Greg asked once, 'Do they know about the film?'

'My parents? Yes. My mother phoned—someone had read it in the paper. Who gave them the story?'

He shrugged. 'Not me. Zuleika, probably. She needs the publicity to help get the funding. So—what did your mother say?'

'I didn't give her the chance to say much,' Eloise told him. 'I said we'd talk about it when I get there. They're not going to like the fact that I've given up my job to write the script, and ...'

'And?'

'And ... a lot of things.'

He laughed. 'Does it matter? Are you really going down there to explain yourself to them, to justify your decisions about your career?'

'I don't want them to be worried or unhappy on my behalf, that's all.'

'If they love you, they'll go along with whatever you want for yourself, and be happy for you.'

'It seems so simple to you——'

'Not to you, obviously. Sometimes I'm glad I have no family.'

She said tartly, 'If you did have one you might be more tolerant and understanding.'

'I'm working on it,' he said, and she threw him a puzzled glance.

They came to a garage and a cluster of shops, with

tearooms and a dairy-takeaway.

'Did you have breakfast?' he asked.

'Just a cup of tea and a piece of toast.'

'I'd like to stop for a snack,' he said. 'Shall we eat here or get some sandwiches to take away?'

There were two families in the small tearooms, with a cluster of young, noisy children.

Eloise said, 'It's too hot to sit inside. Let's picnic.'

Greg bought sandwiches and canned drinks, and some fruit pies, not letting her pay for anything. When she protested, he said, 'We'll put it down to expenses. This trip comes under the heading of research.'

They found a pretty spot off the road, overlooking a stream, under the shade of some prickly totara and yellow-flowered matai. Greg took a rug from the boot of the car and spread it out. She chose to sit at the edge of the shade, where the sun filtered through, and he propped his back against the bark of one of the totaras and opened the packet of sandwiches. Half-turned away from him, she reached for a sandwich, as he did the same, and their hands touched. She snatched hers away.

Greg slowly sat back without taking his sandwich. The tension was knife-edged. Eventually he said, 'I promised, didn't I?'

'I'm sorry. I can't help it.'

He moved suddenly, and she made a great effort of will to stay as she was, but her hands curled in her lap, clutching at each other.

He sighed. 'Give me your hand,' he said.

Eloise looked up without moving.

'Give me your hand,' he repeated, holding his out to her. 'Please.'

Slowly, she raised a hand and put it in his outstretched one. For a moment he just let it lie there. Then his fingers gently closed about hers. 'There,' he said. 'I'm not hurting you, am I?'

'Of course not.' His fingers felt warm and strong and very vital.

'Is my touch—repulsive?'

She looked up then, fleetingly, finding his eyes very steady on hers, his face tense. In his eyes she saw a question, and just the merest hint of doubt. He was less sure of himself than he pretended.

'No,' she said.

His mouth curved faintly. 'I'm glad of that, anyway. You had me wondering for a while.'

'It doesn't mean——'

He said, 'I know. It doesn't mean you're giving me any rights. I won't take anything for granted. I won't kiss you or touch you unless you've made it clear that you want me to. But you might as well know now, I don't intend to let you go.'

Her mouth felt dry. 'You talked about a divorce ...'

'Yes, I did. I asked you what you thought about it. And you said you didn't care, one way or the other. Let's play truth or consequences. Did you—*do* you care?'

Her hand moved slightly in his, and he tightened his hold, just a little, taking care not to hurt. But his fingers were very strong.

'If we're playing truth or consequences,' she said, 'what about you?'

'Haven't I just told you? I love you.'

Eloise shook her head. 'You talked about keeping me—not letting go,' she said pointedly. 'As though you want to own me. Is that love?'

Under the tan his skin went pale, and his mouth hardened. She could see his brain racing, his eyes becoming a focus of light on her face. 'It feels like love,' he said.

Her mouth curved bitterly. 'I want something better than that.'

'Better?'

'Yes. Something more—generous.'

She made to remove her hand from his, but he still held it. 'You haven't answered my question,' he told her. 'What about your feelings?'

She stared down at the red pattern on the rug. 'I don't know,' she said. 'I don't know what my feelings are.'

'You said you hated me.'

She raised her eyes. 'Sometimes I do.'

'And sometimes . . .?'

'I don't know,' she repeated. 'I'm confused—and angry, and——' she moved her free hand helplessly.

'You've been hurt,' he said. 'I know that. I want to make it up to you. I know now that I can. Let me.'

Anger stirred. 'You can't make it up to me, Greg. There's too much that—that can't be made up, can't be "fixed" just like that. You think you can walk in and take over and everything will be fine. Well, it isn't like that. You don't understand, you don't know——'

'Don't know what?'

She shook her head, turning away from him, and he released her hand and grasped her shoulders. 'Tell me!' he said.

'Let me go, Greg. You promised——'

His hands fell away. 'All right. All right, but I want to know.'

'Oh, for God's sake!' Eloise snapped, her emotions overwrought. 'Can't you ever think of anything but what *you* want?'

He sat back and stared at her, and a slow flush rose

along his cheekbones. 'Is that how it seems to you?'

'Yes, if you must know. That's exactly how it seems. That's how it's always seemed. You want me—you want to make love to me—now you want to know what I think, what I feel, what's happened to me—why? Because it gets in the way of what you want from me, that's all!'

His eyes were alight with anger. 'I want to know because I *love* you, and I don't want you to be unhappy.'

'I don't think you have a clue what love is all about,' Eloise said. 'I don't think you ever have. You're an emotional cripple.'

'*I* am?'

'Yes, you!'

'And you? How many years have you been living like a nun, Eloise, with your emotions all safely locked away, rusting from disuse?'

'Oh, you'd like to think it was like that, wouldn't you—that I've been living in some kind of limbo—what were you going to do? Wake me with a kiss? I don't need that, thanks. As a matter of fact, I was perfectly happy without you!'

'Were you?' he demanded.

'Yes!'

'Then why,' he asked with deadly intent, 'didn't you tell me to go when I gave you the chance?'

Her teeth clenched, she said, 'You know why!'

He smiled then, his eyes narrowing. 'Yes, I do. And so do you, though you won't admit it.'

'You always come back to that!' Eloise scrambled to her feet and walked away a little, her arms hugged around her. 'A moment of weakness, if you must know—to put it bluntly, I hadn't had sex in a long time and you were—available. Available and persuasive. It could have been almost anyone, only you happened to be there and that was—convenient.'

Greg had got up too, and was standing behind her. She could feel the tension in him, the self-control he was exerting over himself not to touch her, not to take out his anger and frustration physically on her.

She said, 'Well, you asked for it.'

He didn't answer, and she clamped her lips shut, knowing she had said more than enough. She breathed very quietly, waiting, afraid to move. And then the tension gradually eased, and she knew he had moved away.

'Do you want an apple pie?' he asked, and she almost laughed. It wouldn't do, though, she was still too keyed up, and laughter might end in some kind of hysteria. She shook her head. 'I've had enough. I think I'll go for a walk.'

She still hadn't looked at him, and she started to walk upstream, along a track worn by sheep in the cool springy grass. Mechanically she skirted a gorse bush and pushed aside the branches of a manuka that had fallen across the path, leaving a lingering spicy scent on her fingers. There were ferns growing on the bank. Some of the leaves were blood-red, dipping into the water that raced along its shallow bed, jumping and spurting over the stones in its way. She came to a crossing where stepping stones led to the other side, but didn't venture on to them. Instead, she sat down on a large, flat grey rock and put her chin in her hands and stared at the moving water until she was semi-hypnotised, able to think of nothing much at all.

It was a very soothing pastime, and it was some time later when she reluctantly moved. She got up and turned to retrace her steps—and found Greg leaning against a tree, his arms folded, his eyes thoughtful.

'How long have you been there?' she asked, startled.

'A while. Are you ready to go on now?'

He sounded very polite, and she tried to match his tone. 'Yes, of course. I'm sorry if I kept you waiting.'

'Not at all.' He stepped back rather elaborately to let her pass him; she was terribly conscious of his eyes on her all the way to the car.

When they arrived in the town, Greg parked the car in the wide main street and looked about at the veranda'd shops and the two-storey wooden buildings, many of them refurbished, their nineteenth-century decorative architecture emphasised by judicious painting. 'Yes,' he said, 'it has the atmosphere, all right. Do you mind if we take a walk?'

They strolled down the street, and then climbed a steeper one into the residential area. Modern houses had been built alongside old cottages and more ambitious old villas, one with a small tower on the top.

'I like those things,' Greg said appreciatively. 'We must see if we can include it in a shot.'

'My parents are expecting me for lunch, remember. I'll phone them.'

'I'll get you there in time. There's no need to phone.'

'They'll fetch me if I phone. You want to look round further——'

'Tomorrow will do. Anyway, I can do some exploring on my own later this evening, when I've found a hotel. It'll be cooler then, too.'

Eloise opened the window when they got back in the car, and he said, 'There is air-conditioning.'

'If you don't mind,' she said, 'I prefer the real thing.'

He grinned. 'I guess I'm picking up American habits.

I'd forgotten how Kiwis distrust such luxuries as air-conditioned cars.'

'I don't think that's the right word. Our air isn't polluted.'

'There's more to the States than pollution and fast cars.'

'I know. You like it there, don't you?'

'Some. There are things about home that I miss, though.'

They turned on to a narrower road, that soon became winding and unsealed, the pongas and ladder ferns along the verge coated with grey dust. Then there was a glimpse of water, and he swung the car down into an unkempt parking space by a deep bend in a clear river, with a waterfall soughing into it. Several teenagers, some Maori and some Pakeha, were swimming in the deep pool gouged out by the river, and clambering up on to the rocks of the waterfall to jump or dive in.

'Yes,' Greg murmured, 'I'd just about forgotten that places like this still exist. You used this in the book, didn't you? In the chapter about the swimming party before the men went off to war.'

He pushed open his door, and she followed suit. Walking down to the water's edge, he looked about, his eyes eager, assessing. 'The picnic can be over there,' he pointed to a grassy flat paddock overhung by weeping willows and backgrounded with dense native bush. 'And we'll use that rock the kids are diving from.'

Eloise nodded, wiping perspiration from her hairline with her forefinger. 'Actually,' Greg nodded thoughtfully at the boys and girls splashing in the water, 'that's not a bad idea.'

'Using the rock?'

'Going for a swim. Do you have a swimsuit packed in your bag?'

'Yes, I do.'

'And I keep one in the car. How about it?'

The water looked inviting. It would be nice to arrive refreshed and cool instead of hot and sticky.

'Ten minutes, then,' she agreed.

She changed quickly behind a clump of bushes, emerging in her sleek black satin one-piece to find Greg already in the water. He went under and glided smoothly below the water for several yards, then came up with a shake of his head to smile at her. 'It's cold, but good,' he said.

He was right about the cold, but after the first shock had worn off, she found the water exhilarating. She did a fast crawl across the pool and then turned over to float on her back, looking up at the blue sky. The teenagers were packing up, all of them piling into a battered van, and driving off with a roar of smoky exhaust and some exuberant yells.

'Do you think we frightened them away?' Greg asked, surfacing nearby.

'They didn't look easily frightened to me.' She turned over and began a leisurely breast-stroke, heading for the rocks near the waterfall. Climbing out, she looked up at the higher shelf from which earlier the boys and girls had been jumping.

Greg hauled himself up beside her, and sat on the rock dangling his feet into the water. 'How long since you jumped from there?'

'Are you daring me?'

'I never dare people.' He began climbing. She watched him for a few moments, then followed, her feet easily finding well-remembered hollows and footholds that she had traversed hundreds of times as a child.

He put out a hand to her as she reached the top, and unthinkingly she took it and allowed him to pull her up the final steep slope.

He retained his hold on her hand, and smiled at her, taking a step closer to the edge. The water looked further away than she remembered, and for a moment she almost recoiled. But Greg still had her hand in his. His brows lifted a little, and he said, 'OK?'

'OK,' she nodded, a little breathlessly. It was a long time since she had climbed like that.

He looked a question, and she nodded again, and then they stepped forward together and launched into space, dropping feet first into the water, still hand in hand.

The cool translucence closed over them, blotting out the world in a shell of silence and smooth weightlessness. Their toes touched bottom, then they were kicking upward, and Greg had turned her so that they held both hands, their bodies coming together as they broke the surface, gasping and laughing. His arms went round her, she could feel his legs moving, his thighs against hers. His eyes looked another silent question, and she remembered dreams like this, and closed hers.

She felt Greg's hand brush her cheek, and his voice say, 'Eloïse? Open your eyes, darling.'

Reluctantly, she did so, her body floating with his in the water, his gentle movements keeping both of them from sinking.

She closed her eyes again, but he had seen the answer in them. Her lips parted, and when they felt the touch of his, she didn't protest. Their mouths were cool, moistened with the fresh water, but his kiss was warm and probing, and after a while they both sank under the water until they had to breathe. He pulled her back to the surface, ran his hands along her arms, and released her.

She had no towel, but he let her use his first, and she combed out her hair while he dried himself and dressed.

They got back in the car, Greg tossing the rolled up towel into the back. He paused for a moment, looking at her, and she looked back with a hint of embarrassment. He put out his hand and touched a finger to her lips. 'Don't look like that,' he said softly. 'You haven't given anything away, and I won't take advantage. But it was nice, wasn't it?'

A brown and white dog greeted them at the gate, and ran barking beside them all the way to the square, iron-roofed farmhouse with its veranda along the front. Eloise opened her door, and said sternly, 'Down, Ranger! *Sit*, and be quiet!' When he obeyed, pink tongue lolling ingratiatingly, she patted his head and pulled at his silken ears, saying, 'There, good dog.'

'Eloise!' her mother's voice said. 'There you are! We thought you couldn't have got the bus, or you'd have phoned by now.'

She turned, almost reluctant to meet her mother now that the moment was at hand. 'I got a lift,' she said, as Greg got out of the car and slammed the door shut behind him.

'Hello, Mrs Dalton,' he said.

She stared at him, and was still staring as her husband emerged on to the veranda behind her.

'Greg brought me down,' Eloise explained for her father's benefit. 'I told him I could phone from town, but he insisted on driving me all the way.' She left the dog and walked around the car until she was standing at Greg's side.

Her father directed a searching look at her companion, and said, 'Hello, Greg. Well, you'd better come inside.'

Greg said smoothly, 'I won't intrude on you, thanks. I have to find a hotel for the night, anyway, so I'll be heading straight back to Thames.'

Mr Dalton said, 'A hotel? What for? Of course you'll stay with us. You should have told us you were bringing him, Eloise.'

'It was only last night that we made the arrangement.'

'Well, now he's here,' her mother said, 'he'll have to stay, I suppose.'

Eloise flushed, and Greg, with a sardonic look at her mother, said, 'That really isn't necessary.'

'You can't stay in a hotel,' Mrs Dalton protested.

Greg looked faintly amused. 'I don't see why not.'

'It wouldn't look right at all.' She paused and said, 'You can have the spare room.'

Her husband cleared his throat and said, 'I should think he would be sharing Eloise's room, Jean.'

Mrs Dalton's cheeks grew red and her mouth pursed ominously.

Eloise shook her head vehemently. 'No—we won't be sharing a room.'

With a tremor of laughter in his voice, Greg said, 'Darling, why ever not? After all, we are still married, aren't we?'

CHAPTER SEVEN

'WE are still,' Eloise said distinctly, 'separated. I'll make up a bed for you after lunch.'

She went up the steps without looking at him, and Mrs Dalton said grudgingly, 'Well, you'd better come in, then. I'll lay an extra place.'

She turned and stalked inside ahead of them, followed by Eloise's father. Eloise had reached the coir doormat, automatically wiping her feet, when Greg caught at her arm. 'I can still find that hotel,' he said. 'Unless you want me to stay.'

Oddly, she didn't want him to go. Perhaps all along she had subconsciously been counting on his moral support, even though she knew that his very presence was an irritant, particularly to her mother. 'It's all right,' she said. 'I don't mind you being here.'

'Not good enough, Eloise. Be honest. Would you rather I went away?'

She found the courage to meet his eyes. 'No. I want you to stay.'

He smiled, his thumb moving on her bare arm. 'But in the guest bed?'

'Yes.'

He took his hand away from her arm. 'So be it,' he said.

Lunch was an awkward affair. Mrs Dalton served cold meat and salad, scones and tea in dour silence, refusing help from Eloise. Mr Dalton made stilted conversation with Greg, and Eloise crumbled her scone in her fingers and wondered if it would have been wiser to let Greg go back to Thames.

Afterwards he went out to get their bags from the car, and when he returned she was putting clean sheets on the bed in the spare room. He put down the bag and watched her as she worked. She could feel his eyes on her as she bent to turn down the top one. Straightening up, she said sharply, 'You could help!'

He laughed softly. 'Just looking. You don't grudge me that, surely?'

It seemed churlish to suggest that she did, and yet his looking bothered her. She didn't answer, but turned to put on the bedspread, efficiently tucking it under the pillow and then stepping back. 'There's a towel and facecloth on the chair. If you need anything else, just ask.'

He raised his eyebrows and said, 'I might try it.'

She cast him a frosty look and went to walk past him. His arm barred the doorway, and he said, 'Loosen up, Eloise. I'm only teasing.'

'I'm not in the mood,' she replied shortly. 'Let me pass, please.'

He moved aside, and she went to her own room to unpack.

Eloise scarcely understood her own reactions. She had wanted him to stay, and now she was nervous, on edge. Ever since Greg had come back into her life, she had been on an emotional see-saw. She had told herself that she hated him, and yet when she saw him again, all the force of the attraction he had for her returned, precipitating her into bed with him that very first night, making her waver in her determination never to let it happen again, seducing her into letting him kiss her this afternoon, making her invite him into her home even though her mother's hospitality was so reluctantly given, and she was well aware that her father, too, had no high opinion of him.

She sat on the bed for a long time after she had taken her night things and a clean dress from the bag, knowing she should emerge, but stupidly afraid. There were her parents to be faced. She didn't look forward to making explanations, but eventually it must be done.

When finally she emerged it was to find her mother in the kitchen, fiercely scrubbing potatoes at the sink. Eloise took another brush from a drawer and began to help. 'Where's Dad?' she asked.

'He's gone down to fix the tractor. Greg went, too.'

'Greg?' She didn't think Greg knew much about tractors, but she supposed that he had thought her father's company might be marginally less uncomfortable than her mother's. Stan Dalton's disapproval of Greg had always been tempered with a pinch of male understanding.

Her mother said grimly, 'Yes, Greg—your *husband*. The one you forgot to tell us you were bringing with you.'

'I'm sorry, I should have warned you. But I—I suppose I was embarrassed. And I did intend to have him drop me off in Thames.'

'You mean you hoped we wouldn't know?'

Eloise winced at the accusing tone. 'No, I would have told you. And there are things I have to tell you, anyway.' She wished Greg was here—a cowardly thought, but she knew her mother was going to be difficult.

Dropping a potato into the large pot on the sink counter, Mrs Dalton picked up another. 'You're not together again, are you? You said you're still separated.'

'No, we're not together. This is a business trip for

him. You know about the film—well, we're looking for places to shoot it.'

Her mother scrubbed vigorously. 'You're playing with fire, you know.'

'I'll be careful,' Eloise mumbled.

Mrs Dalton snorted. 'Careful! You've always lost your common sense whenever that man was around. He wants one thing and one thing only. I don't know why you could never see what he was really like.'

'I know what he's like.'

Her mother cast her a dubious look. 'I wonder.' She picked up the pot of potatoes as Eloise dropped the last one into it, and began rinsing them at the sink. Over the sound of the running water, she said, 'He never had any sense of responsibility. I warned you that first time . . .'

'Yes, I know you did.'

'And you were far too young to know what you were doing——'

'Yes, well, there's not much point in going over that again, is there?' Eloise said desperately.

'I suppose not.' Mrs Dalton turned off the tap and returned the pot to the counter. 'But what are you doing now? What *is* all this about Greg directing the film of your book?'

'He's very good, Mum. Probably the best New Zealand has ever had.'

'Who picked *your* book?' Mrs Dalton asked.

'Well—Greg brought it to the attention of the company.'

'I see,' said Mrs Dalton. 'So it was all his idea.'

'In the first place, yes, but you know, there are others involved. The producer, for one. I can't help being thrilled that they chose it.'

Her mother suddenly smiled, though it didn't entirely remove the worried frown from between her brows.

'Yes, dear, of course you are,' she said. 'And your father and I are pleased for you. But—I wish it didn't mean you getting tied up with Greg again.'

'Well...so do I. But I'm not likely to get a chance like this again. I couldn't pass it up because of personal ... difficulties.'

Mrs. Dalton sighed. 'I suppose not. Well, I dare say it'll all be a flash in the pan, anyway, in the end. I mean, it's very exciting and all that, but—films!'

'Greg's done rather well out of them, you know,' Eloise said. 'Directors are very highly paid.'

'Obviously. I saw his car. Spends all his money on that kind of thing, I suppose.' Drying her hands on the floral apron tied round her waist, Mrs Dalton added, 'And you have to write the script?'

'Only because I'd rather,' Eloise explained. 'The offer was made to me, and I took it. I prefer to do it myself, since it's my book.'

'How are you going to have the time? It must be quite a task.'

Eloise took a deep breath. 'I've given up my job—my library job—so that I can spend all my time on the script.'

As she had expected, her mother's reactions ran the gamut of shock, dismay and disapproval. By the time the men returned, the worst of it was over, and Eloise was both relieved and surprised to gather that Greg had told her father all about it. She also noticed that her father seemed to have thawed somewhat towards Greg, and was almost friendly.

After dinner that evening, Greg offered to help her when she volunteered to do the dishes while her parents watched television in the lounge. She said, 'You don't have to, if you'd rather watch too.'

'If you want to get rid of me, say so.' He began

running hot water into the sink, adding a generous squirt of liquid detergent. 'I hoped that the atmosphere here might be a couple of degrees warmer.'

She smiled wryly. Certainly her mother's attitude was cold, her hostility barely disguised by a thin layer of politeness. 'I thought you and Dad were getting on rather well this afternoon.'

'Better than I expected. We had a bit of a chat.' As she turned to him curiously, he added, 'Don't ask me what was said, because I have no intention of telling you. Not that there was much, really. A man of eloquent silences, your dad. What did your mother say about your news?'

'Just about what I expected.'

'I suppose she had a few thoughts on me, too.'

'I'm not going to tell *you* what was said, either.'

'I can guess. I've never been exactly her ideal son-in-law.'

'Poor Greg! You aren't accustomed to being disliked, are you? It must have been a shock to your ego.'

'It doesn't happen too often,' he shrugged. 'I could at least partly understand your parents' feelings in the early days. As far as they were concerned I was just an idle layabout without enough sense to come in out of the rain.'

'Well, they can't say that now, can they?'

'I don't think Stan would. I'm not sure about your mother.'

'Let's leave my mother out of this,' Eloise said swiftly.

'Can we? I want you back, I've told you that. And—if your mother has as much influence with you still as she did before, that's going to make it difficult.'

'Do you think I have no mind of my own?'

'You were never able to stand out against her.'

'Greg, you're obsessed with this! And you're being very unfair. Of course my mother was concerned about us—she and I are very close——'

Greg said, 'Huh! The understatement of the year!'

Eloise flung down the tea-towel she was using. 'I refuse to discuss this! We'll just be going over old ground, and that's utterly futile.'

He said, surprising her, 'You're right. I hadn't meant to bring it up at all. Maybe it's being back here, there is a sort of *déjà vu* about it. Actually, I came filled with good resolutions. I was going to do my renowned impersonation of the perfect son-in-law.'

Eloise suddenly dissolved into laughter. 'You!' she said, still laughing. 'You don't have a hope!'

He watched her, a gleam of humour in his eyes. 'You could give me credit for trying.' He put the last dish in the drying rack and pulled the plug, then wiping his hands, came towards her. With his palms flattened on the bench, trapping her, he said, smiling, 'And what about you, Eloise? Do I have a hope with you?'

Her laughter died. She looked into his eyes, with a mixture of longing and fear. He had charm and charisma, and there was ambition there, too, not the kind that her parents had ever understood, but the kind that had driven him to take a course they thought irresponsible and ridiculous and just an excuse to indulge himself in foolish pipe-dreams. And his gamble had paid off magnificently. But he was not to be relied on. And yet she loved him. In her heart she had to acknowledge that.

'I—don't know,' she said. 'I can't answer that.'

'That means there is hope,' he said. 'At least you haven't turned me down flat.' For a moment longer he stared into her eyes. The laughter had left his face, and he looked intent and serious. His eyes shifted to her mouth, and then back again. 'Eloise,' he said softly, 'I want very much to kiss you.'

She should say no, she knew. She should stop him. He had told her she had the power. She tried to shake her head, but it wouldn't move, and her mouth trembled instead of denying him. Her lips were dry, and she moistened them with her tongue. Something leaped in Greg's eyes, and his head lowered, gradually, until his mouth met hers.

He explored her mouth gently, insistently, his hands still on the bench at either side of her, only their lips touching. Swift and hot, desire coursed through her, and her mouth opened under his, inviting, inciting him. The kiss became deeper, more invasive, and she lifted her hands, feeling him shudder suddenly as her palms pressed against his chest, warm under the cotton shirt.

His hands left the bench and drew her to him, her body pliant against his encircling arms, curved into his as he shifted his feet, parted his legs slightly, let her feel the hardness of desire.

She had to clutch his shoulders to keep her balance, and then her arms wound round his neck, and she was drowned in sensation, the touch, the taste, the feel of him, the scent of his skin, faintly sweaty, but with a musky sweetness. He ran one hand down the length of her body, gathering her even closer, and she cried out, the sound stifled by his mouth.

Greg lifted his head, then bent to kiss her throat, his mouth open on her skin, his tongue tracing little circles. His voice muffled, he said, 'Eloise—I don't want to sleep in the guest bed tonight.'

She took a ragged breath. She didn't want him to, either. She wanted him, needed him, in *her* bed.

Then her mother's voice called from the passageway, 'Eloise? Eloise! Come and see, quickly!'

As if she had been shot, Eloise recoiled, shoving herself away from him, her hands frantically trying to cool her burning cheeks, and straighten her hair.

Greg cursed under his breath. Mrs Dalton called again, nearer now.

'Coming,' she managed to say. 'We're coming, Mum!'

Greg gave a crack of laughter, catching her eye. She clamped her teeth tightly and went towards the lounge with him following. He said in her ear, 'Her timing's impeccable, as always.' Eloise ignored him.

The anthology in which one of Eloise's short stories had appeared had won a literary prize, and Mrs Dalton had called her to watch the news item about it. When it was over, Greg said, 'Congratulations. I haven't seen the anthology. Do you have a copy?'

'There's one on the bookshelf, there,' Mr Dalton pointed out. 'And another in Eloise's room. Help yourself.'

Greg said, 'Thanks.' Eloise carefully avoided his eyes. After a moment he got up and began looking along the bookshelf.

Mr Dalton said, 'You're a clever girl, Eloise. We're proud of you.'

Her mother leaned over, patted her shoulder and kissed her. 'Congratulations.'

'I'm only one of the authors,' Eloise protested. 'And one of the more minor ones, I might add.'

'It's still an achievement,' her mother said loyally.

'I second that,' Greg added quietly. 'She's a very talented lady.'

Mrs. Dalton looked at him with faint surprise. 'Well, I'm glad you realise it,' she said.

Her husband protested mildly, 'Jean!' And Greg laughed. 'I always have realised it, Mrs Dalton,' he said. 'Don't you remember, I wanted her to give up her job years ago, and devote her time to writing?'

Mrs Dalton snorted genteelly. 'Putting romantic notions in her head about starving in a garret!'

'Not exactly. A house-truck, I had in mind. Rather a nice one.'

'And how was she supposed to concentrate, racketing round the countryside in one of those things?'

'Well, it's all water under the bridge now,' Mr Dalton said hastily. 'Our girl's doing very well, and you, Greg— you haven't done so badly for yourself, after all.'

'Thanks.' There was a dry note in his voice. 'I can't seem to find that book.'

'Oh,' said Mrs Dalton. 'I remember now, I lent that copy to someone a few weeks ago.'

'I'll get the one from my room,' Eloise said, starting to rise.

'No, no!' Greg crossed the small space between them and stopped her with a hand on her arm. 'Later will do.'

She caught the look in his eyes, and couldn't stop a flush rising in her cheeks. His hand brushed down her arm before he moved away and resumed his seat. She saw her mother looking at her anxiously.

Eloise had showered and was getting ready for bed when there was a tapping on her door, and it began to open immediately. Snatching up a silky blue robe, she was still pulling it on when her mother came into the room.

'Oh, it's you!' she said.

Mrs Dalton smiled. 'Yes, dear, of course it's me.'

Of course. It had become almost a ritual when she was visiting, that her mother would slip in for a private chat before going to bed herself.

'Greg's in the shower,' Mrs Dalton said. 'I'll take that book and pop it in his room, if you like.'

For an instant, Eloise was tempted. Greg would never know who had put it there, and it would be a clear message that she didn't expect him to visit her room tonight. Because now that she had gained some time to think, she wasn't at all sure that she wanted him to.

But it would be a cowardly way out. And if he did happen to see Mrs Dalton delivering the book, it wouldn't improve their relationship.

'No, it's all right,' she said firmly. 'I'll give it to him.'

Her mother's lips pursed. 'If you're sure . . .'

'Yes.'

The older woman sighed. 'I hope you know what you're doing . . .'

Smiling wryly, Eloise confessed, 'Actually, I don't. I'm very mixed up, but—Mum,' she said gently, knowing that it had to be said, 'I'm an adult now, and I have to make my own decisions, right or wrong. I appreciate that you're concerned about me. Only I can't come running to you for advice every time I strike a sticky patch in my life.'

'Of course you can! We're your parents—you can rely on us——'

'Yes, I know. And I'm grateful. But this is something I have to work out myself. Some decisions no one can help with—no one should.'

Her mother's eyes suddenly grew apprehensive. 'You're going back to him, aren't you?'

'I don't know,' Eloise sighed. 'Oh, Mum—try to understand. I told him today that I was happy without him, but I'm not. I haven't been. I've got over that first horrible, miserable time, but since then I've been only half alive, and didn't even realise it. And now—I'm like a person on a ferris wheel—swooping up to the heights and then plunging down again to earth level, going round and round and not able to get off. I even feel physically sick sometimes with the—the speed of what's happening to me, the excitement of it. I know it's a risk, but maybe it's a risk I have to take.'

Her mother sniffed. 'Sex! That's all it is. He's hypnotised you with sex. Just like before.'

Eloise shook her head. 'I haven't explained very well. That's a part of it, yes, but it's more than sex. It's being with someone who has—I don't know—a kind of *energy* for life. He's always made me feel stimulated—mentally as well as physically. Most of my best stories I wrote when I was married to him—living with him. Even the novel . . . I wrote the first draft in note form before he left, and though at the end we weren't happy together, his presence, just his being there, still kept my mental adrenalin going.'

'You can't trust him!'

Slowly Eloise said, 'Maybe not. But I think I may need him.'

'Oh, *Eloise*!' Her mother's eyes were wet. 'He made you so unhappy.'

Eloise put her arms around the other woman. 'Don't! Please don't make yourself miserable. Don't worry about me. I will sort myself out.'

Pulling a hanky from her pocket, Mrs Dalton sniffed into it. 'I suppose so. I just wish you'd remember——'

'I do,' Eloise assured her patiently. 'Believe me, I haven't forgotten a thing. And inside, deep down, I'm still angry with him, still raging. I don't know if I can overcome that, and if I can't—then perhaps there's no hope for us, after all. If I can't forgive him, then—we might only destroy each other. But maybe I was too unrealistic, expected too much. He said—he said I was carrying round a mental picture of some perfect man, and that he didn't measure up, that nobody could. Perhaps he's right.'

'Dear, you just built him up in your mind into some kind of hero . . .'

'Yes. And he wasn't. So maybe I should accept that I married a real man with real faults, and give our marriage another chance. Anyway, nobody can help. Not you, not anyone. This is between me and Greg.'

Her mother cast her a glance of despair. 'I can't help being worried, you know.' She sighed. 'But I'll try not to interfere.'

A light tap came on the door. Mrs Dalton hastily wiped her eyes, and pushed the handkerchief back into her pocket.

Greg opened the door and stood in the doorway. His hair was wet from the shower, and he had put on a black towelling robe. His eyes slipped over Eloise, and his mouth curved very slightly at the corners. Then his gaze moved to her mother, and the curve straightened into a hard line.

'Mrs Dalton,' he said, with an ironic inflection.

'I just came to say goodnight to Eloise,' she said. Her hand was curled around the hanky in her pocket, and her voice was flat.

He nodded, and came into the room, and stood holding the door for her. 'Goodnight,' he said pointedly.

Eloise cast him a look of anger, and her mother, after a moment's hesitation, walked past him without speaking.

Greg closed the door behind her with a snap, then turned and leaned against the wood with his arms folded. His eyes were narrowed and glittering. 'And what,' he enquired, 'did your dear mother have to say besides goodnight?'

CHAPTER EIGHT

'DON'T you sneer at my mother!' Eloise flashed, instantly on the defensive.

'I wouldn't dream of it,' Greg said, lifting his brows. 'I have the greatest respect for the lady—she's certainly managed to change *your* mood.' He looked around the room. 'She didn't take her broomstick, has she left it here somewhere?'

It was too much. The ferris wheel had plunged again, and with a vengeance. Right now she couldn't understand why she had ever loved him; he was being pigheaded and unreasonable and—plain *jealous*, she guessed, just when she had persuaded her mother to keep out of their affairs and at least try to reconcile herself to the thought that they might renew their marriage.

She turned away from him and took up the anthology that lay with some other books on the bedside table. 'This is what you came for, isn't it?' she asked distantly, as she faced him and held it out. 'So please take it and go.'

He came away from the door slowly, the expression in his eyes threatening. She would have stepped back, but the bed was behind her.

He took the book and turned it over, looking at it. Then he raised his eyes again to her face, and his mouth twisted.

'No,' he said, tossing the book on top of the bed. 'This isn't what I came for, and you know it. Your mother knew it too. That's why she came in here, dripping poison, no doubt. Trying to talk her darling daughter out of sleeping with her lawfully wedded husband!'

'It wasn't like that, and you have no right——'

'Oh, I'm sure she didn't put it as crudely as that—and I have every right! She made good and sure we broke up before——'

'That's not true—and you know it isn't——'

But he overrode her, not listening. 'And I'm damned if I'll let it happen again. That's why I insisted on coming with you. At least, if I'm here, I can try and see she doesn't have it all her own way——'

'Will you *shut up*!' Eloise cried, her rage overflowing, mingled with a strange, tearing pain that the promise of today, the tentative understanding with her mother, had ended in this jeering, hurtful tirade.

'All right,' he said, tight-lipped. 'Perhaps I should do as you suggest—take what I came for, and go.'

As his hands came up, she drew back one of hers and slapped him, very hard, jerking his head aside and back. She tried to run then, to get past him, but he caught her and threw her roughly down on to the bed and pinned her there with his body. His anger, she saw, matched hers, his breathing already quickening, his lips drawn back in a grimace that was almost a snarl as he grabbed at her flailing hands and held them in a painful grip.

'I'll scream!' she panted.

His face was inches from hers, on his cheek a scalding mark where she had hit him. 'Scream, then,' he invited softly. 'The way you used to when we lay here together like this, and you'd scream, "Yes, yes, like that, don't stop, please don't stop," and hide your face in my shoulder so that your parents wouldn't hear. I swear I still have the marks of your teeth on my skin.'

As he lowered his head, she sobbed, '*No!*' But he took her mouth with his, taking advantage of her parted lips, forcing her mouth open, sliding his tongue between her teeth, the tip of it grazing the roof of her mouth, moving back and forth.

She closed her teeth, but his grip tightened on her wrists, and he shifted one hand to her hair, swiftly gathering it up with a threatening tug. She didn't dare to bite him, but exerted all the will-power she had to refuse him a response. Her body lay rigid beneath him, her mouth suffering his invasion without reciprocating.

After a long time, he lifted his head, looking down at her, his eyes narrowed and very blue and hard. She was on fire all over, consumed with a brilliant mixture of rage and unwanted desire.

'Why don't you give in, Eloise?' he asked her softly. His eyes dropped, lingering on the swell of her breasts, the little shadow between them where the robe she wore had loosened. He ran a hand down over the silk, possessively, shaping her breast, her hip, her thigh, then sliding back to her waist. 'Come on, darling, you want it, too ... You do, don't you? Admit it, there's nothing to be ashamed of.'

He leaned down and put his lips to her skin between the lapels of the robe. His mouth burned, seared. His hand came to the opening and his fingers slid inside the fabric. She stiffened, squirming under him, shaking her head.

'Don't,' he said, lifting his mouth. His hands moved to her head, his fingers tangling into her hair, holding her so that she had to look at him. 'Don't be silly.'

His voice caressed her, but his hands were strong, even though he wasn't hurting her in any way.

She said, her voice raw, 'I can't stop you. It won't be

the first time, will it?'

He was very still, looking down at her, his eyes burning into hers. The flush of desire on his face faded, leaving his skin strangely pale and drawn. 'You can stop me,' he said, 'with one word.'

Her mouth opened, her throat working as she tried to force the sound through dry lips. His eyes wouldn't let her go, and she closed hers to blot out the blazing desire, the accusation in them. And finally she managed, scarcely more than a whisper. 'Go.'

Sunday was unseasonably grey and cool, with spurts of misty rain that blotted out the hills beyond the farm. At least the weather matched her mood, Eloise thought. She went to church with her parents and returned to find Greg standing on the veranda, looking grim and with his hair and clothes damp.

'I went for a walk,' he explained. 'There seems to be a sheep in trouble, Stan, in one of the back paddocks. I wasn't able to catch it, but it's limping, and I think it has some barbed wire around a leg.'

'I'll check it out.' Mr Dalton began to remove his jacket as he went into the house.

Turning, Greg asked, 'Could I help?'

The look on Mr Dalton's face said that he doubted it, but he answered, 'If you like.'

They were away for over an hour, and when they returned the two women were making lunch. As much as possible, Eloise avoided looking at Greg at all. They left early in the afternoon, and as she waved her parents goodbye she knew that she faced a couple of hours alone with him in the confines of the car.

He drove in silence for a while, and then said, 'Well, as the return of the prodigal son-in-law, that was hardly an unqualified success.'

'Do you care?' she asked. He had never given her any reason to suppose he was affected either way by anyone else's opinion of him.

'Yes, I do,' he said unexpectedly.

'I don't see why,' she muttered, staring out of the window. 'You certainly never gave a damn before.'

'I care because it's important to you,' he said deliberately. 'And this is *now*, not "before". It's a different ball game.'

'Is it?' Eloise allowed her scepticism to show. If this was different, there was a depressing sameness about recent events.

'At least your father seems willing to suspend judgement.'

'Then you might do the same for my mother.'

He inclined his head as though conceding a point. 'I'll do my best.'

'She promised not to interfere—just before you came into my room last night.'

He hid his reaction quickly, but she had already seen the cynical disbelief in his expression. 'Oh, what's the use?' she cried.

'I haven't said a word.'

'You don't need to. I can see what you're thinking.'

'All right, then. No comment.'

Greg was looking straight ahead, his lips firmly shut, and she sighed with exasperation and closed her eyes, pretending to sleep. She knew there was some justification for his sceptical reaction, in the light of the past, but he was overreacting. If her mother had interfered before, she had done so with the best of motives, and not without some reason. When Greg first came into her life, Eloise had been very young—only seventeen. And her parents' anxiety had been perfectly natural.

Greg Stone, twenty-two years old, had dropped out of university two years before without finishing the science degree he was studying for, to travel with a group of friends overland through Australia, Asia, Africa and Europe. In a succession of four-wheel-drive vehicles they had careened about the world living from hand to mouth, taking temporary jobs where they could get them, falling into one hair-raising adventure after another, and filming it all with a second-hand movie camera which they shared along with everything else. They had hoped to sell the result, perhaps to television, after the film had been edited and had a commentary added. One of them, who had done a little work in television, assured the others that the idea had commercial possibilities, but on the way home through the Middle East, there was trouble at a border, and nervous police, apparently convinced they were some kind of spies, threw them into prison overnight and confiscated the camera and all the carefully preserved films.

'We never saw the gear again,' Greg told Eloise, when he relayed the story to her. 'The next morning they opened the cell door, quite literally kicked us out into the street, and more or less threatened that if we made any kind of trouble we'd go back in again for a very long time. They threw our passports after us, and a couple of rucksacks of clothing and books that they'd taken from the Land Rover the day before, but the camera and all our films were missing.'

'And you couldn't get them back?'

'We tried, but they got very nasty, and in the end we had to give up. The country was on the verge of a pretty bloody civil war, and the consulates were being evacuated. We only got out by the skin of our teeth, in the end. The road was bombed behind us.'

It all sounded incredibly exciting to Eloise, and the bearded, tanned stranger dressed in a tartan shirt, shabby jeans and heavy boots who had come into the library looking for books on movie-making was even more so. After helping him sort through all their small stock on the subject, she had been pleased but hesitant when he asked her if he could spend her lunch break with her.

He grinned at her and said, 'I'm sorry I'm not dressed for a fancy restaurant, but I've found a coffee bar that has good food, and it's clean. So am I, under this gear.' He fingered his chin. 'I'd have shaved if I'd known I was going to meet someone like you.'

It wasn't the first time she'd been complimented, she couldn't help knowing she was pretty, but he seemed more worldly-wise than the few young men she knew and the grin made her realise that he was extraordinarily handsome beneath the beard. She liked him already, for they had briefly discussed the books she had found for him, and he had shown intelligence and a sense of humour. She smiled back and said, 'Thank you. I'd like to come.'

Over lunch, he told her the story of his travels, and when she asked, 'What are you doing in Thames?' he laughed ruefully.

'Jobs are hard to get. And since the idea of the film didn't come off, I had to find some way to live. I was labouring on a building site when I met a guy who reckoned there's good money to be made pig-shooting in the Coromandel. There's quite a growing market for wild pork in some of the tourist hotels. A couple of us decided to try it. He may have been right, but I'm not very good at it. I was thinking of packing it in and going back to Auckland.'

'Has something changed your mind?'

'Yes.' He wasn't smiling. 'Meeting you.'

Eloise searched his eyes. They were blue and steady, and he looked as though he was serious. Uncertainly, she said, 'You can't mean that.'

'I don't say things I don't mean.'

She shook her head slightly, looking down at her plate. He said, 'Does that mean you don't want me to stay around?'

'No, it doesn't!' she said emphatically, looking up at him. Then she blushed, but he just laughed in a soft, pleased way, and said, 'Can I see you tonight?'

'I'm—not busy.'

'Good. Then what would you like to do? Dinner? A film? There's a good one on at the moment, I noticed.'

He was interested in films, of course—the pile of books he had taken from the library lay on the table at his elbow.

'A film would be nice,' she said.

'We'll have dinner first. Or supper after—or both—so that we can talk.'

Eloise laughed. 'We'll go Dutch, then. You can't afford all that.'

'Yes, I can. I've just sold a couple of pigs. That's what I'm doing in town. When I'm broke, I'll let you know, and it can be your turn to shout.'

The assumption that they would be seeing a lot of each other made her a little breathless, but she managed to say with a smile, 'All right. I'll hold you to that.'

They settled on supper. Eloise was glad that she would have the chance to make herself look her best before he collected her in time for the film.

Her parents had been slightly scandalised that her date

for the evening had, as her mother said, virtually picked her up. 'It's nothing like a pick-up,' Eloise protested. 'I met him at work, that's all.'

Her mother sniffed, and her father looked doubtful and said, 'Well, we'll see what he's like when he comes to get her.'

Eloise prayed that Greg would not turn up in the clothes he had worn that morning, but for all she knew he had no others. Well, she would go anyway, she promised herself, as she put on a pretty blouse and a full skirt with its own wide buckled belt. She was sure he was a perfectly safe escort, and besides, it wasn't often that someone as exciting as he was entered her life. She didn't intend to miss out on an interesting evening—and the prospect of more to follow—because her parents were over-cautious and old-fashioned.

When he arrived, she saw that he had trimmed the beard, revealing that she had not been mistaken about his looks, and although he still wore jeans, they were new jeans and his denim shirt and tan dress boots were new too. He must have spent the afternoon shopping. He seemed faintly amused at her father's hard scrutiny and her mother's leading questions. As he answered, his voice seemed more drawling and less cultured than she remembered, and his face was very bland. Far from trying to set their minds at ease, he seemed bent on presenting an image of a slightly uncouth ne'er-do-well, purely for his own amusement.

She enjoyed the film, and even more the discussion that followed over a late supper. He knew so much more about the technical details than she did that after a while she laughed and said, 'You don't need those books you got this morning! Why are you so interested?'

'I don't know,' he said. 'I got fascinated by the

techniques of filming on the trip I told you about, when we all had a go with the camera. I've been thinking since I got back—that's what I really want to do. Make films.'

Incredulous, Eloise laughed again. 'Just like that? What sort of qualifications do you have?'

He grinned. 'None. Except what I learned from filming "Our Trip".' He put the mock title in quote marks with his fingers in the air, so that she pictured the words on a family photograph album or at the beginning of a home movie. She laughed. 'You can't even show them that! It's lost.'

Greg laughed too. 'But that's what I want,' he said. 'To be involved in film-making. And you?' he asked her. 'Are you dedicated to library work?'

Then, although she seldom talked about it outside her family, she confessed her ambition to be a writer.

'You sound almost apologetic about it,' he said. 'Why?'

'Well—you know,' she said awkwardly. 'People think it's a little—odd.'

'It's not odd,' he said. 'It's terrific. Are you any good?'

'I don't know. I've had a couple of pieces accepted, in magazines, but more have been returned with rejection slips.'

'I'd like to read some.'

'You can read the published pieces. Not the others.'

'Why not the others?'

'Well—I just feel shy about them, that's all. No one reads them except my mother.'

'I see. Is she a good critic?'

'Oh, she's no critic!' Eloise grinned. 'She thinks everything I do is wonderful. It gives me the confidence to send them out to an editor!'

* * *

'What are you thinking about?' Greg asked now, slowing the car as they approached a bend in the road where a few sheep were peacefully grazing outside the fenced farm paddocks.

'Nothing,' Eloise said.

'Congratulations,' he said drily. 'That's quite a feat.'

'Nothing important, then.' Stupidly, she felt guilty. Of course their first meeting had been important. It had changed both their lives.

He glanced at her. 'I've been thinking about this film. In your story, when the man goes to war, and has to kill other men, you have this thought going through his mind about pig-hunting back home—he tries to deny the reality of what he's doing by comparing it with hunting wild boar.'

'Yes.'

'Well, it's quite a telling point. And important to later developments, too. But we can't convey his thoughts— at least, not a specific thought such as that—to the audience.'

'Well—dialogue?'

'How? Are you going to have him turn to the man next to him as he shoots and say, "Hey, this is just like shooting Captain Cookers back home in li'l ole Noo Zillan"?'

Eloise smiled in spite of herself. 'I'll be more subtle than that. Maybe there could be some discussion among the men, about their feelings. He might bring it out as a sort of justification.'

'No.' Greg shook his head. 'I can't see it working. In film, you show it, don't tell it. We'll have to film a pig-hunt.'

Eloise said instantly, 'There isn't any hunt in the book.'

'I know. But the thought goes through his mind——'

'Only fleetingly. It's over in a second.'

'An important second. It's the only way to make it work, don't you see? We need a quick cut to show what he remembers in the instant he squeezes the trigger—the climax of a pig-hunt. And it won't make any sense to the audience if they haven't previously seen the original scene—the chase and the kill.'

'I hate the idea!'

'I don't much like it myself. But you can see it's necessary. Nothing else would work as powerfully in terms of images.'

'Surely . . . there must be another way.'

'Think of one.'

'Well . . .' she said doubtfully, 'I suppose we could fake it.'

'That would be difficult to do convincingly.

'I won't have some poor animal killed just so that we can make a film look realistic! It's revolting! I'm sure the SPCA wouldn't allow it.'

'We can send a camera team out with some hunters and get the footage we need, and slot it in. The actor's part can be faked to some extent. Especially if we can get one of the hunters to look something like him, and wear the same clothes.'

Upset at the prospect, she said resentfully, 'You'd do anything to get a good piece of film, wouldn't you?'

'Almost,' he admitted. 'But I don't particularly want to stage a special pig-hunt.'

He had not enjoyed his own hunting days. When he told her he wasn't very good at it, Eloise had thought he meant that he had trouble finding and killing the animals. But it wasn't that. He had, he'd said, been sickened by the whole business. The hunters used dogs and a knife, although most carried a rifle for emergencies, and the wild boars were armed with formidable tusks. The risks had at first appealed to him, for a tusked boar was a cunning and dangerous adversary when cornered, but the frequent bloody battles between dogs and pig until the hunter was able to close in with his long knife and slit the pig's throat resulted in both animals frequently being badly mauled. Greg had given it up, soon after he and Eloise met, and had for a time been unemployed.

Not having the 'stomach' for pig-hunting had confirmed Stan Dalton's suspicion that there was something wrong with Greg Stone. And being unemployed had strengthened Mrs Dalton's conviction that he had no staying power and no ability to hold down a steady job.

To the Daltons senior, the world-ranging trip he had made with his friends was proof of instability and irresponsibility, especially since he had interrupted his education to do it. They were unimpressed by the tales of adventure that Eloise found fascinating, and the range of jobs he had held for short periods overseas and since his return. Although Eloise had discovered that his marks at university had been high before he decided that genuine education was to be gained in the real world rather than in books and lectures, Mrs Dalton insisted on characterising him as a 'failed student'. Nothing Eloise said could change her mind.

Greg had never lived down the first impression they had gained of him, had never attempted to. Mrs Dalton was icily courteous to him and made it quite clear, as he amusedly told Eloise, that he wasn't fit to lick her daughter's dainty shoes. Mr Dalton regarded him with barely concealed contempt and had never failed to ask him, when he called for Eloise in his borrowed transport, whether he had found a job yet.

'They don't mean it,' Eloise said, a little troubled, as they drove away from the farm one evening. 'They don't know you very well, that's all. And you must admit, you're not helping much.'

'Helping?'

'Well, you do put on that lazy dole-bludger act for them.'

'Act?' he said innocently. 'What act?'

'You know perfectly well,' she said. 'You deliberately make them think you're not interested in working.'

He laughed. 'What on earth makes you think that I am?'

She hesitated, then said firmly, 'You're too energetic to not want to do *anything*, even if you're choosy about what it is. And too independent to want to rely on government handouts. You're just taking a holiday, now—a breather while you contemplate your next move, that's all.'

He looked at her with something verging on respect. 'The thing is,' he said, 'I have no idea what my next move is going to be.'

She was silent for a few minutes. 'I wish you *would* find a job,' she said, rather wistfully. 'I know it's none of my business, but——'

'But——?'

'Oh—nothing. I am right, aren't I? You don't really want to be unemployed for ever.'

'Does it matter?'

She shook her head. Of course it didn't matter. She believed in him—didn't she?—no matter what her parents' opinion. And anyway, Greg was a free agent. He wasn't answerable to either Eloise or her mother and father for what he did with his time. It wasn't as if he had a family to support. 'It's nothing to do with me,' she said hastily.

Greg looked at her shrewdly and said under his breath, 'Or your mother.'

A few weeks later he said to her, 'I'm going back to Auckland. Will you come with me?'

They were lying side by side on the beach, prone in a sheltered little nook between enormous rocks. The sun struck sparks off the sand and the sea rushed and rippled over a scattering of tiny coloured pebbles before hissing into a series of white bubbles near their toes.

Eloise's heart gave an odd little lurch as she said, 'Come with you? What do you mean?'

He raised his head, giving her an amused look, then he smiled and put out his hand to touch her cheek. His eyes suddenly tender, he said, 'We could get married.'

'*Married?*' Eloise twisted suddenly and sat up in a flurry of sand.

'Why not?' He sat up too, more slowly. 'Wouldn't you like that?'

'Yes!' she said. 'But my parents would never let me!'

For weeks she had been living in a bubble of joy, seeing Greg at every opportunity, spending her evenings, her weekends in his company, talking, walking, watching films, swimming and sunbathing, laughing— and kissing. She knew her parents didn't like her seeing him, and Greg knew it too. He never said anything, his manners when he met them were almost too impeccable, but the laughing glint never left his eyes.

Pushing aside the small shadow on her happiness,

ignoring her mother's occasional critical remarks about Greg's clothes, or his hair, which she considered over-long, or his continuing lack of employment and self-admitted disinclination to look for any, she had lived from day to day, deliberately not thinking about what might lie ahead.

Greg said, 'We'll just have to talk them into it.'

But of course it was hopeless. She was not even eighteen, her parents had never liked him, and he had no money and no prospects. 'You must understand,' Stan said impatiently, 'it's nothing personal. But no parent is going to allow a daughter of that age to marry a fellow without a job, without a home to offer her, without any hope of being able to provide one.'

Greg gave him a long look and said, 'If I get a job—and a home—what then?'

Stan said, 'Well, we'd have to see.'

Her mother said swiftly, 'She couldn't possibly! Anyway, she's far too young.'

Greg's gaze went to her thoughtfully, and then to her husband. He put out his hand to Eloise, who was sitting beside him, tense and pale, and she put hers into it. Her fingers were trembling, and his clasp tightened almost painfully.

'We can be engaged,' she said, 'can't we?'

Greg looked at her quickly, and his eyes suddenly narrowed.

Mrs Dalton snorted. 'He couldn't even afford to buy you a ring! Can't you see, Eloise, this is just puppy love!'

Eloise started to protest, but Greg said, 'No, no engagement.'

Stunned, Eloise turned to him, her eyes wide and hurt.

He didn't explain anything, just said curtly, 'Well, we

know how you feel. Thanks for making it so clear. If you'll excuse me, I'll be on my way. Eloise, will you see me off?'

She went with him, out on to the veranda and down the steps to the Land Rover he had borrowed from his pig-hunting friend. Her hand was still in his, and she looked at his face and saw that it was hard and almost expressionless.

Her own emotions were strangely mixed. She felt bitterly disappointed and terribly surprised that Greg hadn't fought harder. She had somehow expected him to be able to win out over all opposition. He had always given her the impression that if he tried, he could do anything. Perhaps deep down her mother recognised that quality too, for she had said several times that if he really wanted a job he could have got one.

'What are we going to do?' she asked him forlornly.

He looked down at her, his expression brooding. 'Would you come with me, anyway?' he asked.

A ripple of fear ran through her. Swiftly, he said, 'We could still get married. It takes about three days to get a licence, I think.'

'It wouldn't be legal, would it?'

'You'd have to lie about your age, but they'd have to take us to court to do anything about it afterwards.'

Eloise felt sick. 'I—I couldn't,' she said. 'I can't do it like that. It would break their hearts. Greg—why can't we be engaged? I'm sure I can talk them round, eventually. And if we were committed to each other, however long it takes——'

He said roughly, 'Because they're right. You *are* too young.'

Stung, she cried, 'Well, why did you ask me to elope, then?'

'To see what you'd say.'

Snatching her hand from his, she said, 'You mean you were *testing* me? Well, I'm sorry I got the answer wrong!'

He grasped her shoulders, then pulled her close and covered her lips with his, kissing her with a kind of desperate hunger he had never shown before. And Eloise kissed him back, heedless that her parents might see. Nothing mattered but the fact that Greg loved her, wanted her. They would work this out somehow if she could persuade him to be patient.

He wrenched his mouth away and buried his face against her neck, his arms still tightly holding her. 'It's no good, honey,' he said. 'It won't work.'

'It would work,' she said, the tears starting to trickle down her cheeks, 'if you loved me enough.'

He lifted his head, and smiled crookedly at her, wiping the tears with his thumbs. 'Or if you loved me enough,' he said. 'If you're honest, you'll admit you were relieved when your parents said no.'

She opened her mouth to deny it, but he put a finger over her lips, firm and warm. 'It's true. I saw the look on your face. You're not really ready to marry me—that's why you wanted an engagement, a breathing space.' She pulled away from his finger, but he stopped her passionate denial with a quick kiss on her parted mouth. 'It's OK.' His fingers were not quite steady as he smoothed back her hair, his eyes devouring her face. 'Don't cry. They're right about one thing—you're too young. I should have realised it. What we've—had—has been wonderful, Eloise.'

She made an inarticulate sound, and clutched at his shirt front, frightened by his talking in the past tense. 'Don't say that! As though it's all over——'

But he went on ruthlessly. 'I don't want this to turn sour on us—and it would.'

'How could it? I love you!'

'With me in Auckland, and you here with your parents——'

'We can write to each other—phone—we'd have some weekends together——'

'Do you think that they would allow that? And they'd have plenty of time to feed those doubts of yours.'

'I wouldn't listen. And even if they don't give their consent, we can still be engaged! They can't stop us promising each other——'

He shook his head. 'Half a loaf? No, thanks.'

Eloise at last drew away from him, paling as the implications sank into her mind. 'You're letting me down lightly, aren't you? You never wanted to marry me at all. You just said that because you didn't think I'd go with you if we weren't married, and now you're glad to be out of it! You're not worried about me at all! You just want to be free to find some other girl who will give you what you really wanted all along! Well, go ahead. I don't care!'

She turned to flee into the house, but as she reached the top step of the veranda, Greg caught at her wrist, and she was jerked back, and down into his arms. His face was hard, his eyes glitteringly angry. She drew a startled breath, and then his mouth found hers, relentlessly. She struggled against him, suddenly frightened, tears burning her cheeks, her throat raw and her chest feeling as though it would burst.

When he let her go, she was speechless, and his face was white under his tan. 'Goodbye, Eloise,' he said, and in two strides had reached the Land Rover and leapt into the cab. He turned the key and swung the vehicle down the drive, going fast, without looking back.

Eloise, running back into the house, brushed by her mother, who followed her into her bedroom. 'Oh, my dear,' she said, as Eloise flung herself, sobbing, down on the bed. 'He isn't worth it, believe me.' Eloise felt a gentle hand stroking her hair. 'There, dear, you'll get over it. I know you think your heart is broken, but you're young yet. There'll be other young men—better ones.'

Her mother had been proved partially right, at least. There had been others, but none as interesting, as vital, none who made her blood sing with a touch, or sparked desire with a look, or added a new dimension to her life just by being there. None like Greg Stone.

CHAPTER NINE

TWO years later she met him again, and nothing had changed.

In Wellington to complete her library training certificate with a six-week intensive course at library school, Eloise had been walking along Lambton Quay, buffeted by one of the city's notorious gusty winds, even though the sky glimpsed between the tall buildings lining the street was a clear pale blue. Not having mastered the art of walking head-down into the wind without colliding with other pedestrians, she was dodging a large woman with a child in tow, chilled fingers clutching at the edges of the jacket she wore over a summer blouse and skirt, when a hand on her arm stopped her and a well remembered voice said, 'Eloise!'

He had shaved off the beard, but she would have recognised him anywhere. His voice, his eyes, were just the same, and in the short time she had known him before, his personality had been indelibly stamped on her psyche. She stared at him dumbly, until someone bumped into her with an impatient apology and he said, 'We'll find somewhere to talk.' He steered her into a coffee bar, dimly lit and aromatic, with a dark red carpet on the floor and imitation brass lanterns on the walls. 'Coffee?' he asked, and she nodded, telling herself she ought to get up and walk out. It was frightening the way she felt—her pulses jumping all over the place, adrenalin flowing, every sense registering twice its normal awareness level. When he sat opposite her at the small table, she could smell the masculine aroma of his skin, her fingers aching to touch him. She couldn't help revelling in the sight of him, the clean-shaven chin, as square and uncompromising as she had known it would be, the dark hair cut a little shorter, tidier than before, the strong, clever hands, the determined mouth that held a slight curve now. He laughed softly, and reached out to cover her fingers with his. A tingling like an electric shock ran up her arm.

Taking a grip on herself, Eloise withdrew her hand smartly. 'We don't really have anything to talk about, do we?'

The look in his eyes changed, becoming wary. 'You could start by telling me what you're doing in Wellington.'

She told him briefly, and he said, 'You're still living at home?'

'Yes.' She took her eyes away from him to stare at her coffee, watching the cream swirl on the top.

'Do you have a boyfriend?'

She looked up at him, and hurt stirred. What gave him the right to ask her a question like that? Trying to sound casual, she answered, 'Several.'

Greg smiled, his eyes examining her as though he was mentally weighing her answer, and she asked, 'What about you? Have you got a job?'

'Not at the moment. I've just finished working on a film——'

'So you did go into films. What do you do?'

'Nothing important—yet. But I'm learning a lot.'

'How long have you been working in the film industry?'

'Off and on for the last two years. I've done some acting, some fetching and carrying, a bit of camera work. In between, I take other jobs to keep body and soul together and fill in the time—or I go on the dole. It's not what your parents would call steady work.'

'You're not married?'

'No,' he said curtly. 'I'm not married.'

She looked away again, holding her cup in both hands as she lifted it, and he said softly, 'Are you glad?'

'It's none of my business.'

'It is if you want it to be.'

She spilled some coffee, and put down the cup to wipe at her hand and the table with a paper napkin. He watched her, and when at last she raised her eyes, it was to find his intent and questioning. 'How old are you now?' he asked her.

'N-nineteen.'

He said, 'I promised myself, when you were twenty I'd find you again.'

'I'll be twenty this year,' she said. She searched his face, afraid to trust him. Her mother had said he would forget her, that men were like that, that he had only offered marriage on the spur of the moment and had no doubt been glad to get out of it. And that the sensible and healthy thing to do was to forget all about him, in turn. First love was often painful, but one learned lessons from experience. It didn't do to trust one's instincts in these matters. Reason was often clouded by emotion where the opposite sex was concerned.

She had come to believe that her mother's advice was soundly based. Greg had given her no reason to think otherwise.

'You don't believe me,' he said.

Eloise shook her head. 'You never even sent me a postcard.'

He put down his cup. 'Where are you staying?'

'In a hostel. A women's hostel.'

'Can we go there?'

Again she shook her head. 'No men allowed.'

He grasped her hand. 'Come on,' he said, pulling her up.

He took her to a hotel room. 'I have to be out of here by tomorrow. The film company is paying for it.' It was small and obviously cheap, and the bed sagged in the middle, but it was clean. 'Don't look so nervous,' he said. 'I didn't bring you here with seduction in mind. It's a private place to talk, that's all.'

He took her jacket, throwing it on the bed. Eloise sat down on the only chair, a straight-backed, hard-seated affair standing in front of a small table that evidently served as dressing table and desk combined.

Greg walked to the window and stood looking out for a minute, his hands thrust into his pockets. There seemed to be nothing to look at but the brick-walled back of another building, but he didn't face her as he said, 'I didn't send a postcard—or a letter—for the same reasons that I didn't want an engagement. It was better to end it then and there, with a clean break. It saved me a lot of slow torture, and you the embarrassment of having to admit you'd changed your mind. There's nothing worse than the gradual disintegration of love.'

She said sarcastically, 'You sound as though you know all about it—I expect you've had plenty of experience.'

He turned. 'More than you have, my love. Certainly more than you had two years ago. You must have grown up a bit since then.'

'Yes. Enough to know that I'm not *your love*. So don't call me that.'

Turning at her hostile tone, he said slowly, 'You still don't see, do you? Well, there's not much point in going over it all again.'

'No, I don't suppose there is.' She jumped up, assailed by a stupid desire to cry, and anxious to leave while she could still control it. 'I'll find my own way out. Don't come down.'

'Your jacket——' he said, as she made for the door.

She wheeled and made blindly for the bed where he had thrown her jacket down, and at the same time he stepped forward to pick it up. Their hands touched, and she snatched hers away. Through a blur of tears she saw him lift the jacket, and tried to keep her eyes on it, reaching out shaking fingers to take it from him. But he didn't let go. In a strange voice he said, 'Eloise? Eloise!' And then the jacket dropped to the floor between them, and he took her groping hand in his, holding it tightly, and with his other hand forced up her chin.

She tried to twist away, biting her lip hard to stifle a sob. He kicked the jacket out of the way and took her in his arms, murmuring her name, pressing kisses on her temple, her cheeks, and at last on her hot, swollen mouth.

She tasted the salt of her own tears on his lips, and gave a long, shuddering sigh, her body melting in his arms, flowing with liquid fire, pliant, wanton. She felt as though she was being given something she had been starved of for far too long.

He groaned and pressed her closer, his hands shaping her shoulders, the curve of her back, the narrowness of her waist and fullness of her breasts. With his mouth against her throat, he murmured. 'You feel so sweet— you do still love me. My God, I've dreamed of this— remembered it so often—the feel of you, the taste of your mouth, the sound of your voice. Tell me you love me, darling. I want to hear you say it.'

Her eyes closed, dizzy with the sweet shock of desire, she whispered, 'I love you, I love you—I always loved you. Oh, Greg, why did you leave me?'

'Shh, not now, darling.' He silenced her cry with his

lips. 'I'll never leave you again, I swear.'

He eased her down on to the bed, the sagging mattress soft beneath her, and his hard warm body pressing on hers, rousing her to an unbearable pitch of desire. She gasped, her mouth opening like a flower under his, allowing him to explore it fully with his tongue, his body deliciously heavy over her. She writhed under him, with a wilful urge to bring him even closer, and he suddenly lifted himself away, leaving her restless and fretful, her eyes flickering open impatiently, wanting him with her. He was smiling, pulling off his shirt, and as she looked at him, his hands went to the buckle of his belt.

A sudden frisson of fear shivered through her, and she closed her eyes. His voice amused, he said, 'Darling, what's the matter?'

'Nothing,' she said, wishing he would come back to her, stay with her, warm her with his body, and drive away the sudden panic she felt. 'Hurry!' she said, her teeth clenched because they had developed an alarming tendency to chatter. As soon as she heard herself say it, a hot wave of shame engulfed her. She thought of her mother, how shocked she would be, how disappointed in her daughter's behaviour.

Greg laughed softly, low in his throat, and said, 'All right, darling. I won't keep you waiting.' Then he was with her again, kissing her throat, his hands sliding under her skirt, arching her to him. He seemed very strong and very big and terrfyingly male. His passion was less tender now, more demanding, dominating. She shivered, and he asked, 'Are you cold?'

Eloise shook her head. She was cold, but not in the way he meant. Her mind was a kaleidoscope of broken thoughts racing through her head. Her mother, Greg, her father, the last time Greg had kissed her, in anger and farewell, the things she had said to him then, and his refusal of what he had called half a loaf. And afterwards, her mother's insistence that it had been only a phase in her growing up, an unimportant episode. And then, today—this. This was not supposed to be happening. Her mother would have been horrified ...

She wanted him to stop her thinking, take her back to the heedless passion of a few moments ago, but though she clutched at his naked shoulders and offered him her mouth again, nothing would stop the clamouring of her brain, and at last it took over and made her body slack and unresponsive. She tried to recapture the mood, but when Greg made to gently part her thighs, she instinctively clamped them together and turned away from him, crying, 'No, I can't—I can't!'

After the first blank silence of surprise, he put a hand on her shoulder, and said, 'Eloise? It's all right, I'll be careful not to hurt you. There's nothing to be afraid of.'

Shaking him off, she jumped to her feet, dragging on her clothes in frightened haste, trying not to look at him. 'It's not that,' she said jerkily. 'I just—don't want to.'

'You really mean that?' He sounded half ironic, half disbelieving.

'Yes.' She couldn't manage any more. What else was there to say, anyway?

She did up the buttons of her blouse with clumsy haste and tucked it into her skirt. After several stunned seconds he got off the bed too, and pulled on his trousers in grim silence. With a vicious tug he fastened his belt. 'Is this some kind of revenge?' he asked her.

Her shocked eyes flew to his face.

'Because if so, it's a dangerous game you're playing,' he said softly.

Finding her voice, she said, 'No, of course it isn't! I couldn't—I *wouldn't* do that.'

'You just suddenly changed your mind,' he said, with a hint of a sneer.

Distractedly, Eloise smoothed her tumbled hair with her hands. 'Please, Greg—I'm sorry. I just—I couldn't go through with it.'

'You just told me you loved me.'

Her lashes swept down, her head turning away. It was one thing to say it in the heat of passion. It was embarrassing to be reminded of it. And now she recalled with brutal clarity that he had not replied in kind. All her mother's warnings reiterated themselves in her mind. Men would say anything when they wanted sex, the vast majority of them were interested in only one thing, but they didn't respect the girls who gave it to them.

'Wasn't it true?' Greg challenged her.

Suddenly angry, she swung round on him. 'Yes, it was true! Are you going to insist that I "prove it" to you?'

A strange expression crosssed his face, and his eyes held a steely light. 'Yes,' he said, 'I am.'

Leaden disappointment lay in her chest, but she held his eyes with hers, her head defiantly up, her mouth tight. 'All right,' she said, her voice full of contempt for him. 'If that's what you want.'

Deliberately, she began to unbutton her blouse. Then Greg said quietly, 'No. Not like that.'

Her fingers faltered and stilled. 'I don't understand.'

His mouth curled. He stepped closer and slowly did up the buttons she had opened. Then, not touching her at all, he said, 'I want you to marry me. Not when you come of age, not when your parents give their consent. Now—just as soon as we can get a licence.'

Her parents, of course, were convinced she had gone mad. Her father threatened to have the marriage annulled, phoning a lawyer for his opinion before he calmed down and accepted the *fait accompli*. Her mother ran the gamut of tears, reproaches and accusing Greg of everything short of rape, but they had been quietly married in a register office in Wellington and had the certificate to prove it. Furthermore, as Greg unblinkingly told them, the marriage had been consummated, and he and their daughter were legally husband and wife.

'I'm sorry we did it without telling you,' Eloise said to her parents, 'but we knew you wouldn't like it, whichever way we went about it. This way seemed the simplest.'

'Oh, yes,' her mother said bitterly, her eyes on Greg. 'He hoped to avoid trouble, no doubt. It was his idea, wasn't it?'

'Yes,' said Greg, 'it was. I talked her into it.' He had actually insisted. She could tell her parents first if she chose, he had said, but if Eloise intended to marry him, it must be immediately. He would not wait. When they got heated over the issue, he finally shouted at her, 'I've lost you once, Eloise! Do you think it was easy, keeping away, leaving you to get on with your growing up, hoping to *God* you weren't meeting someone else that your parents would approve of and talk you into marrying? I nearly went crazy just thinking about it! Your mother isn't going to like me any more than she did then—she'll do her damnedest to stop us.'

'I wouldn't *let* anyone stop us!' She was flushed, shouting too.

'I won't run the risk. Once is enough. Are you going to marry me or not?'

She was almost ready to yell a refusal, when something in his face stopped her. Her eyes were very blue and glittery, with a desperate kind of hunger in them, the skin over his cheekbones drawn and strangely pale, and there was a tightness about his mouth.

And in the end she had given in, seeing without understanding the fear behind his insistence, more than a little shaken by the depth of feeling he had unwittingly revealed.

Mrs Dalton of course saw him as a cradle-snatcher, a ravisher who had taken advantage of her daughter's youth and innocence. 'You knew we'd try and persuade her to see sense,' she said with bitter accusation.

'I knew you'd do your best to stop her marrying me.'

Her father said, 'Well, it's done now. I just hope you won't regret this, Eloise.'

While Eloise worked out her month's notice at the library, they stayed on at the farm. Greg had wanted them to move into a flat or house in the town, but Eloise begged him to reconsider. 'I know it won't be comfortable for you, but it's been a big enough shock for them, my getting married so suddenly. At least let me have these few weeks with my parents while they get used to the idea. Besides, it will be a good opportunity for them to get to know you. After all,' she added, 'you've had it all your own way until now. Please, Greg, give in to me on this?'

He smiled at her wryly. 'All right. It won't make a blind bit of difference. Your mother, at least, is determined to hate me, and all your wishful thinking won't change that. But I suppose it was generous of them to agree to have me—even if your mother did want to put me in the spare room.'

Eloise giggled. 'Poor Mum!' Mrs Dalton had offered the spare room with its single bed to Greg, who had cocked a wicked eyebrow at her and said smoothly, 'No, thanks, Mrs Dalton. Eloise and I will be quite happy in her bed, together.'

Her mother had hardly known where to look, and Eloise herself had blushed fiercely. Surprisingly, she thought she had caught a hint of a smile on her father's face before he had hastily changed the subject.

That night, in the narrow bed she had slept in almost all her life, Greg joined her and took her in his arms. For the first time, when he made to remove her nightgown she demurred, her hands against his chest, whispering, 'I don't know, Greg—I—perhaps not tonight.'

He propped himself on one elbow, looking down at her. 'We're going to be here for a month, Eloise. Do you intend to remain celibate all that time, just because your parents are across the passageway? Because I don't.'

'It's just that I feel——'

'Inhibited? Don't be. We're married. They know it. Good lord, they've been married themselves for how long—twenty-five, thirty years? They know what we're doing, and if we're not doing it, they'll assume that we are, anyway.'

Of course it was silly to feel shy about making love in her parents' house. He was perfectly right. She smiled uncertainly. 'I know. I'm sorry.'

He kissed her, and his hands wandered over her possessively. 'Relax. Let yourself go, honey. That's better. Put your arms round me, touch me—there, yes—and there. You like that, don't you? Do you like this? And this? Does it feel good?'

He talked to her, soothing her in his deep hypnotic voice, but not whispering, unworried about being overheard. And after first caressing her into total relaxation, he brought her gradually to a fever pitch of excitement, and kept her teetering there on the edge, deliberately letting her slide back once, twice, three times, before he brought her to the brink again, holding himself in check with iron self-control, until she was almost frantic with need, sobbing. 'Now, please—*now*!'

She knew that he was close to losing himself, too, but he smiled and said, 'Now—what? Tell me! Go on, say it, tell me what you want!'

Half laughing, half crying with the sweet torture of frustration, she told him, explicitly, and he laughed too, teasing, and said, 'Louder—ask me again. Louder.'

She did, half screaming the words, her fists thudding against his bare shoulders, his chest, and then at last he sent her flying over the edge, spinning, falling in a vortex of sensation, holding him as she cried out again and again, imploring him to go on, on, on . . .

She surfaced at last with her whole body tingling right down to her toes, and her mouth buried in the sweat-damp skin of his shoulder. 'Oh, heavens!' she breathed, appalled, as the darkened world spun into focus again and she could make out the dim shape of the window, the gleam of the polished top of the dressing-table. 'Do you think they heard us?'

She felt him shake with laughter. 'I hope so,' he said. 'I hope they heard everything. Now they'll know that you belong to me.'

Shocked by his blatant admission, Eloise had never again totally lost her awareness of her parents' presence in the house. It became a game, with something more underlying it, between her and Greg. Every night he made love to her with an intensity and purpose that forced the sounds of ecstasy to her lips, laughing at her efforts to stifle her uncontrollable cries of passion. She would deny him the pleasure of hearing them for as long as she could, but when she could hold back no longer, the piercing joy of release was overwhelming. He would watch her, his eyes brilliant even in the darkness, until she lay quiet and exhausted, and then he would slake himself on her, letting his own passion have free rein, giving her a second, different, more diffuse fulfilment.

Greg had offered to help about the farm in the daytime, only to be brusquely rejected by his father-in-law. 'I can manage on my own. I always have. You don't know anything about farm work, anyway, do you?'

'No,' Greg admitted. 'But I'm willing to learn.'

'I haven't got time to teach you,' grumbled Stan. 'You'd be better off finding yourself a job in Thames.'

But they didn't intend to stay in Thames. 'We're moving to Auckland,' Greg said, 'as soon as Eloise finishes at the library. I'm hardly going to find a job that temporary, easily. I thought I might as well make myself useful round here in return for my keep.'

Stan grunted. 'All right, then. I'll be starting early in the morning, mind. Just don't get in the way.'

Greg managed not to get in the way, he told Eloise drily. Stan's manner toward him became slightly less intolerant, Eloise thought, but when he discovered that Greg didn't have a job to go to in Auckland, and that he still wanted to work in films, he demanded to know what on earth they thought they were going to live on.

'I've already applied for a job in a suburban library,' Eloise told them. 'I'm almost sure to get it. And Greg has some savings.'

'You can't live on savings,' Stan objected.

'We don't intend to, Dad. Greg's heard of a film that's due to start soon, and he hopes to get a place in the crew.'

'And in the meantime?'

'We'll live on my wage,' Eloise told him.

Stan looked at his son-in-law with contempt. 'You're willing to let your wife keep you?'

'It won't be for long,' said Greg, a glint appearing in his eyes. 'I appreciate your concern, Mr Dalton, but you needn't worry. I won't let Eloise starve, I assure you.'

'What about these savings of yours?' Stan persisted doggedly. 'How much have you got?'

Eloise said, 'Dad!' But Greg told him. He looked mildly surprised at the sum, but said, 'It isn't enough for a deposit on a house.'

Greg smiled. 'We don't want a house. As a matter of fact, we've been talking about buying a truck with it, after the film is finished.'

'A truck? You're going into business?'

'No, a house-truck. Mobile living quarters.'

'Greg is thinking of making a documentary film about New Zealand,' Eloise explained. 'There could be a market for it overseas. We plan to travel round, filming, and save accommodation costs. The truck would be home and transport. He knows someone who's planning to sell theirs in the next six months.'

'And Eloise could concentrate on her writing,' Greg added. 'Without a nine-to-five job, she'd have more time for it.

'And what will you live on, then?'

Greg shrugged. 'Odd jobs, anything that comes up.'

'And whatever I earn from my writing,' Eloise added.

Stan snorted, and when Mrs Dalton heard of the scheme, she went tightlipped and finally burst out, 'Dragging her round the countryside like some kind of gypsy! Of all the hare-brained schemes——'

Eloise said, 'I'll enjoy it!'

'You'll get travel-sick!'

'Oh, Mum, I grew out of that years ago!'

'You were sick when we went over to Matamata, and you were eighteen then.'

'I'd just had 'flu.'

'What about last Christmas, when we went to that beach where Glenda and Ray were spending the holidays?'

'It was a bad road.'

'And is *he* going to stick to good, sealed highways?'

Greg, looking thoughtfully at Eloise, said, 'I hadn't intended to. I want to cover the backblocks—the people and places the tourists never go to.'

'See?' Mrs Dalton said triumphantly. 'And in a *truck*! You're bound to be sick.'

'I'll take pills,' Eloise said.

'They make you dizzy and send you to sleep. You know that. How much writing do you think you'll get done, then? And supposing you get pregnant?'

Eloise blushed. 'Well, supposing I do?'

'You won't find it much fun having morning sickness, tearing around backblocks roads in a truck, I can tell you!' her mother said grimly.

A flicker of uncertainty crossed Eloise's face. 'Well, I won't get pregnant,' she said bravely. 'I shall just have to make sure I don't.' Greg's plans certainly didn't include a family yet, she knew.

Mrs Dalton snorted and darkly muttered something about the best laid plans, and nature having its way.

Greg put his arms about Eloise and said, 'It's only an idea, Mrs Dalton. Perhaps we should give it some more thought.'

When they were alone, later, in the kitchen after dinner he said to Eloise, 'Why didn't you tell me you suffer from travel-sickness?'

'I don't always.' She hesitated. 'Besides, you were so keen on the scheme——'

He regarded her with a strange expression on his face. 'So you just went along with it?'

'I liked the idea!' she protested. 'And—oh, it's such a childish thing—being sick like that.'

'It was childish not to tell me,' he said. 'I know I'm a selfish swine, but I don't intend to make you miserable just so that I can have my own way.'

'You're not selfish!'

He said, sombrely, 'Don't try and fool yourself, Eloise. You'll only be disappointed if you make me out to be something I'm not. Maybe being brought up without a family of my own, I haven't had to consider anyone else except on a superficial level. Ever since I left school, I've pleased no one but myself. And now—there's you.'

With quick fear, Eloise wondered if he was regretting their marriage. He had been a loner, free to go where he pleased, work or not as he wished. With his upbringing, it wasn't surprising. His father had disappeared to Australia when he was barely four, and his mother died the following year. He had been brought up in institutions and temporary foster homes, and never had got used to being in one place for long. Now he was looking at her as though she was a millstone about his neck.

'You made me marry you!' she reminded him. 'You practically bullied me into it.'

'I know I did. I'm just beginning to realise what I've done.'

Hurt and shaken by the admission, she turned away from him. He laid a hand on her shoulder, but she shrugged it off. 'Eloise?' he said, and grasped her shoulders, pulling her round to face him. Stubbornly she kept her head down and he drew her closer, trying to lift her chin with his hand. Then her mother came into the room, saying, 'Stan wants a beer. He said to ask if Greg would like one.'

Eloise jumped away from him as though caught in a guilty act, and saw his mouth quirk as he said, 'Thanks, I would, Mrs Dalton.' He always called her by the title, punctiliously, a practice which served to emphasise the scarcely concealed enmity between them, and he nearly always responded to her with a hint of humour lurking in his eyes, as though her slightly barbed politeness amused him. Her mother had noticed it, Eloise knew, and was annoyed and even flustered by it.

As she was now. Taking a bottle of beer from the fridge, Mrs Dalton's hands were not quite steady, and she almost droppped it.

Greg rescued the bottle deftly, and placed it on the table. 'Shall I open it for you?' His voice, as always, was smoothly courteous. Eloise never did work out how he managed to make courtesy itself sound insolent.

'Yes, thank you,' Mrs Dalton replied stiffly. 'I'll get the opener.'

'It's OK, I know where it is.' Extracting it from the drawer where it was kept, he removed the cap. The liquid fizzed a little, the bitter, tangy smell of it filling the small kitchen. 'Glasses?' he said.

Mrs Dalton was standing and watching him. 'Yes,' she said, turning to the cupboard. But Eloise forestalled her, taking out two large glass mugs. Suddenly she was obscurely angry with Greg, and had a confused and quite illogical feeling that her mother needed protecting. 'You go back to the lounge,' she said to the older woman. 'Greg and I will bring the drinks in.'

She put the glasses on the table, and Greg said, 'What's the matter, Eloise?'

'Nothing. Pour the drinks, will you?' He filled the glasses, and she immediately picked them up to carry them into the other room. 'You might as well bring the bottle,' she advised. 'I'm sure the two of you can finish it.'

Picking it up, he came behind her as she reached the door, and bent to put his lips to the side of her neck.

'Don't!' she said sharply. And, as he stepped back, 'You'll make me spill the drinks.'

When he followed her into the other room a few moments later, she could read nothing in his face, but as he sipped at the cool beer and then lowered the glass, he caught her eyes and held them with a long, level look that somehow promised a reckoning.

When he slid his arms about her as she stood in front of the dressing-table, brushing her hair, and deliberately repeated his earlier action, kissing her neck, she stiffened a little, because something in the way he held her made it a challenge, a reminder of her earlier rebuff.

His mouth, though, was warm and soft and coaxing, and after a few seconds, he took the brush from her hand, laying it down on the dressing-table, and turned her fully into his arms, kissing her mouth. Eloise made an inarticulate little sound, and soon her arms wound about his neck, her head falling back under his increasingly passionate possession, her body pliant to the needs of his. At last he swung her up into his arms and took her the few strides to the bed, and in the naked light of his desire she knew that if he had doubts, regrets, this at least could quench them.

CHAPTER TEN

THEIR first quarrel had been precipitated by her mother. Mrs Dalton had made the suggestion that while Greg went to Auckland in search of a job and a place to live, Eloise should remain at home with her parents. Greg turned it down flat, with what Eloise considered was unnecessary brusqueness and without even glancing at her, let alone asking for her opinion. 'She was only trying to be helpful,' she told Greg later. 'You could at least have been polite about it.'

'I'm always polite to your mother,' Greg reminded her coldly. 'I even thanked her for the offer. I'm living in her house and I do have a minimum of good manners.'

'A minimum is right!'

His mouth tightened. 'I knew it wasn't going to be easy, living under the same roof with your parents, but it was what you wanted. Only I'm not going to leave you here, and give them the opportunity to talk you into believing that marrying me was a huge mistake! I don't think you realise how much influence your parents still have over you. You looked ready to consider that ridiculous suggestion.'

'It wasn't a ridiculous suggestion!' Even though she had not even for a moment contemplated accepting it, only hesitating so as to frame a lovingly tactful refusal, it wasn't fair of him to be so scathing. Her mother's intentions had been good. 'It was a perfectly sensible idea.'

'For God's sake grow up, Eloise!' he snapped. 'You

have to leave home some time. You've had a month to get used to the idea of being married, and moving out. So make up your mind. Either you're an adult woman and you belong with me—your husband—or you're just a child still, afraid to leave home and your mother!'

Angrily, she had denied it, and the argument had rapidly escalated into a slanging match, until eventually Eloise had gone to bed in stubborn silence. When Greg climbed into the narrow bed beside her, she moved right to the edge, and when he put his arm across her body, curving about her waist, she lay still and unresponsive.

After a moment he gave a vexed little laugh and said, 'Don't be so silly. You'll fall out if you move any farther away from me.'

She didn't answer, and he tugged, bringing her back against him, then moved to turn her into his arms.

She resisted him silently and there was a grim, tense little struggle. He kissed her, angrily at first, and then with a deliberate, controlled attempt at seduction. For perhaps a minute or two she held out, then slow tears trickled from beneath her lids, and she gave a trembling sigh against his mouth.

He lifted his head. 'Don't cry,' he whispered, kissing the tears away. 'I won't force you. Go to sleep.'

But she clung to him then, stopping his movement away from her. 'I don't want to fight.'

'Neither do I. I didn't mean to hurt you. But I don't intend to lose you, Eloise. You're coming to Auckland with me.'

'Yes,' she said, 'of course I am.'

He didn't give her a chance to say that she had always intended to, or to ask him what he had meant yesterday when he seemed to be doubting the wisdom of marrying her at all. He stroked back her hair with both hands, and holding her face gently between his palms, began kissing her again, with fire and purpose, and after a while explanations didn't seem important.

They moved to Auckland and found a flat, furnished it as cheaply as they could, and Eloise began work in a library, being put in charge of the children's section. At night she worked on her stories, finding the ideas flowing. She was given an extra impetus by Greg's encouragement, even though she seldom let him read her work.

Greg contacted the people who were supposed to be filming the screen version of a recent New Zealand best-seller, and said they were to start shooting in three weeks. He visited the labour department, but temporary jobs were few and far between. So when her mother and father visited them, Greg was 'unemployed' again. Eloise could see that they were sceptical about the film. Her mother said tartly, 'The trouble with that young man is he thinks life's nothing but a game.' As they left, her father pressed a twenty-dollar note into her hand.

She showed it to Greg later, making a joke of it, but he didn't laugh. His face went taut and he said, 'All right, the hell with the film ... tomorrow I'll get a job.'

'I didn't mean that——'

His face softened a little. 'No, I don't think you did. But I find I don't much like the idea of being a kept man.'

He found jobs, all kinds of jobs, none of them career-orientated, and her parents continued to disapprove. Then the chance came of a place in a directors' course aimed at training people to work in television, and they used what was left of their savings so that Greg could take it. He wanted to work in feature films, rather than television, but the training and the experience would help. Afterwards he was offered a job with the television corporation, and Eloise proudly reported the fact to her family. Greg directed one segment of a current affairs programme, and then was dropped from the payroll.

'*Why?*' Eloise asked. The disappointment was sickening.

Greg shrugged. 'There was a disagreement over how the programme should be done. I couldn't do it their way.'

She tried to understand, but the anti-climax was tremendous. For the first time, she began to let the doubts surface that she had suppressed ever since their marriage. Her mother's tight-lipped criticism, her father's quietly sceptical attitude towards their son-in-law, had, almost without her realising it, undermined her confidence in him. It seemed that he had had his chance to start on the ladder of success in the difficult career that he claimed to be aiming for—and he had deliberately blown it for a doubtful principle.

Some time later when a small argument had developed—now she didn't even remember what had started it—and he had made some laughing remark in the middle of it, she had flung at him in temper, 'My mother is right about you! You don't take anything seriously, do you?'

He was sitting at the kitchen table, tipping his chair on its back legs. He didn't move and didn't answer, but the laughter left his eyes abruptly. 'Do we have to bring your mother into this? Interesting as her comments on my character undoubtedly are, it's been rather refreshing since we left Thames to be free of her dragon-breath down my neck every time I turn around—and to know she's not listening outside our bedroom door at night.'

'That's a foul thing to say! She never listened outside our door, and you wouldn't have cared if she had.'

He laughed, and let his chair down. 'No, I didn't give a damn, but you did. You never willingly let yourself go. If we'd stayed there much longer you'd have become frigid. Was it the thought of your mother that made you suddenly become so inhibited, in Wellington?'

She couldn't stop the betraying flush rising to her cheeks, and he laughed again and got up, coming towards her. 'It was! Talk about the long arm of the law—what about the long tongue of the mother-in-law!'

He tried to take her in his arms, but she pushed away from him.

'Not ready to kiss and make up?' he asked, smiling at her.

'You think that will solve everything, don't you? Don't you ever think about anything but sex—and films?'

'I'm not thinking about films now.' He rocked slightly on his heels, his eyes slipping over her, a half-smile on his lips.

'You're not even serious about that, really, are you?' she challenged him furiously. 'All this talk about films is a pipe-dream, a convenient excuse to avoid having to commit yourself to a proper job.'

The smile disappeared and his eyes hardened. 'More quotes from Chairman Mother?' he asked silkily.

'*And will you stop jeering at my mother!*' she shouted. 'I don't need her to tell me that I've married——'

His eyes narrowed. 'What?' he said very quietly. 'You've married— what, Eloise?'

Appalled at the thoughts that had surfaced, driven by anger up from her subconscious, she whispered, 'I didn't mean it. I was angry.'

Now she wanted him to take her in his arms, to blot out the doubts, the fears. But he didn't. He stood looking at her for a long time, his face quite unreadable. And then he said, 'I'll be back later,' and walked out of the house.

He had got a job with a trucking firm, driving long-distance lorries. 'They wanted full-time, long-term staff,' he told her. 'I told them I was available.'

'You don't have to——'

'It's what you wanted, isn't it?' he asked her, his eyes daring her to contradict him. 'It may not be good enough to satisfy your parents, but it pays well, and I'm damned if I'm going to be tied to some bloody office all day!'

Sometimes he was away overnight, or even for several days, and she spent much of her spare time writing. Most of what she sent out came back, with terse rejection slips attached. But some had encouraging personal notes added by the editors, and now and then one sold. She started a journal of jottings and notes and some diary entries, with a vague notion that one day she would write a novel. She didn't tell Greg about it.

Their savings mounted again, and Eloise began to be hopeful that one day they would be able to afford the deposit on a house of their own, and perhaps start a family. Once on her afternoon off she went down to the trucking office in her lunch hour to take him a registered letter that had arrived at the house, thinking it might have been urgent.

He tore up the letter, saying briefly, 'It's nothing.' He looked around for a rubbish bin and, not finding one, stuffed the pieces into his pocket. A few days later she saw him take the torn letter from his pocket and smooth it out, then crumple it quickly and toss it in the waste-paper bin by the dressing-table.

'What is it?' she asked.

'Nothing,' he said, as he had before. 'It isn't important.'

'If it isn't important, you can tell me what it is.'

'It's a job offer. And I've already got a job.'

At Christmas they spent two days at the farm. Eloise thought that her family were on the verge of accepting Greg at last. But she couldn't help noticing that he seemed increasingly irritable. She put it down to the weather and the long hours he worked, but when she suggested that he didn't need to work quite so hard, he turned on her and snapped, 'We need the money, if we're going to have that cosy little dream home of yours.'

Hurt, she said, 'You don't want it, do you?'

He looked at her and his face softened. He took her chin in his hand and lifted her face, kissing her gently. 'Whatever you want,' he said. 'That's what I want for you.'

He was not always so tender. Sometimes his lovemaking had a quality of near-desperation, so fierce and unrestrained that it almost frightened her. And sometimes they quarrelled equally fiercely. In fairness Eloise had to admit that her temper flared easily these days—it seemed that all her emotions were heightened by living with Greg. He seemed always barely in control of some pent-up anger and frustration. Even his teasing had frequently an underlying cutting edge to it. There were times when she was starkly aware that something was very wrong.

At the beginning of February she came in quite late

after shopping on Friday night. As she put away some groceries in the kitchen, she heard raised voices, and wondered who Greg had with him.

She went into the lounge to find Greg on his feet, his stance aggressive, as he said forcefully, 'I told you, find someone else. I'm not available!'

The other man was seated on their second-hand sofa, lean, clever-looking hands peaked under a bearded chin. 'You're the one I want,' he said. Then, seeing Eloise in the doorway, he rose to his feet. 'Mrs Stone?'

Greg said, 'Yes. My wife. Eloise, this is an old— acquaintance of mine. Basil Blakeney.'

Shrewd brown eyes looked into hers. 'I'm trying to persuade your husband to join me in a business venture,' he said. 'He's a hard man to get hold of—doesn't answer letters, even registered ones. I thought, the only thing to do is come and see him in person.'

Eloise said, 'What is this business venture, Mr Blakeney?'

'I'm starting a film company,' he said. 'A co-operative company. Greg has experience in both films and TV, and that's important, because we want to make features, but also we can do independent film-making for sale to the corporation, and there's a lot of bread-and-butter in that.'

'There's no point in telling her all this,' said Greg. 'I've already said, I'm not interested.'

Eloise looked at him, saw how tense he was, his jaw so tightly clenched a muscle twitched in his cheek, his eyes glittering and his mouth a straight, harsh line.

'Perhaps you can change his mind?' the man said hopefully to Eloise.

'I—it's Greg's decision,' she said uncertainly. 'Greg——?' He wasn't looking at her but at Basil

Blakeney, as he said, 'Go on, then. Tell her the rest. Give her the bottom line.'

'Well, Mrs Stone, it's like this. We can get a certain amount of financial backing, if we can raise the balance ourselves. As I said, it's a co-operative. So everyone in the company invests some money.'

'How much?' Eloise asked.

Greg answered for him. 'All of our savings. Plus a few hundred more that we'd have to borrow from somewhere.'

Eloise went pale.

'We can't afford it,' Greg said. His voice was harsh, with an underlying mockery. 'Sorry, Basil, you'll have to try someone else.'

After he had gone, still protesting that it was Greg he wanted, and surely there was some arrangement they could come to, Eloise turned to Greg. 'Is he a con man?'

'Nothing like that. He's an experienced producer, with plenty of clout in the financial world. The thing will probably work.' He was walking restlessly about the room, not looking at her, touching an ornament on the table, picking up a book and putting it down again.

She was sure there was more risk than he suggested. She knew that films always cost vast sums of money and often made little or no profit.

'You want to do it, don't you?' she said quietly.

He looked up, briefly, and she was rocked to the core by the expression in his eyes, the blaze of hope, almost a kind of hunger. She hadn't seen him look like that since they had argued in Wellington about getting married without waiting for her parents' approval, the only time he had revealed briefly his naked need of her.

'Of course I *want* to do it! It's the chance of a lifetime, that's all. But don't worry, I've given all that up.'

'For me?'

He moved his head, a strange little gesture that was neither a shake nor a nod. 'For our marriage. You'd resent like hell having our money go into a gamble like that, when all you really want is a cottage with roses round the door and kids playing on the lawn.'

He hadn't been able to quite hide the bitterness in his voice. She said huskily, 'And what about what *you* want?'

A strange light played in his eyes. 'I want you.'

And she suddenly saw how it would be. It was true that the thought of all their money going into a risky venture made her throat fill with angry tears. And it was also true that if she allowed Greg to make this sacrifice, no matter how well-intentioned, he couldn't help but be angry and resentful about the wasted opportunity. Either way, she saw with sudden dreadful clarity, their marriage didn't stand a chance.

She said huskily, 'Tell Mr Blakeney you accept his offer.'

'You don't mean that.'

'Yes, I do. You once said you couldn't stand the thought of our relationship going sour. Neither can I. Tell Mr Blakeney you accept.'

That blaze of hope came into his eyes again. Her throat felt raw, she wanted to howl, scream, put her arms about him and cling for all she was worth. She clenched her teeth hard, holding on to her emotions.

He came over to her, and studied her face. 'You're sure?'

'Yes. Quite sure.'

When it was done, their money transferred irretrievably to the company and Greg installed in an office in a brand-new film studio with the company's name proudly emblazoned on the façade, Eloise packed her bags, wrote him a note and left.

He came after her, of course, arriving on the doorstep of her parents' home. 'I knew you'd be here,' he said, a hard hand on her arm as he pulled her down the steps and made her walk with him across the lawn. 'Home to mother again. Was she the one who persuaded you to leave me?'

'No one persuaded me. We want different things, Greg. You were the one who said a clean break is better than a relationship going sour. When Mr Blakeney came along, it was time for a clean break.'

He stopped walking and jerked her round to face him. 'You planned this?' he said between his teeth. 'You knew you were going to ditch me, when you said to accept Basil's offer?' His hands bit into her arms. He took a jagged breath, his eyes burning. 'You told me to take it because you knew you were leaving. So you wanted to give me a consolation prize! Well, thanks! I'm deeply moved by your generosity!'

She stared at him, not knowing how to answer. He was putting his own interpretation on her actions. And did it really matter? Nothing they could say to each other was going to make any real difference.

She looked away from him across the drowsing paddocks to the hills in the distance, hazily purple in the sun.

Greg dropped his hands. He said slowly, 'Were you so unhappy?'

Eloise shook her head. 'We were neither of us happy. You know you were stifling in domesticity. It doesn't suit you. You resented it.'

'You're just making up excuses.'

'We'd hardly been married a month when you told me you regretted it.'

'*Told* you so?'

'Don't you remember? You said you were just beginning to realise what you'd done.'

'I didn't mean what you thought.' He was looking at her strangely. 'I'd just realised how young you still were, and what I'd taken on in promising to make you happy. I tried to do that, Eloise. I tried with everything I have— but it wasn't enough, was it?'

'Do you think I wanted my happiness at the price of yours?'

'I *love* you! We can work it out—unless you don't love me enough to want to try.'

'I love you enough to give you your freedom.'

He made an impatient gesture. 'A freedom I haven't asked for and don't want!'

'You haven't asked for it. But you do want it.'

His gaze narrowed. 'Is this some sort of sacrifice?'

'No. It's some sort of salvation, for both of us. Please, Greg. We made a mistake. Let's call it quits before we begin to hate each other.'

He stared at her for a long time in frustrated silence, his brows drawn together, his eyes gradually growing cold. 'Maybe it's already too late for that,' he said. Then he walked away from her, and left without a backward glance.

CHAPTER ELEVEN

FOR several weeks after the trip to Thames Eloise worked long hours on the script, and didn't see Greg at all until she had outlined all the scenes. Aaron, now officially her script editor, said Greg should see it, and the three of them had a script conference. To her relief, no vast changes were made, and Greg treated her exactly as he treated Aaron, with cool professionalism.

Fleshing out the scenes, writing directions and dialogue, took much longer, and meantime Zuleika and Greg were making preparations for the shoot.

The first few scenes were shot in an Auckland studio. Eloise was fascinated to see the chemistry that suddenly developed between the two protagonists on camera, for they showed no sign of being romantically interested in each other offscreen. The male lead, Neville Payne, was an actor who had made a name for himself in Australian television, and the female lead had just returned from working in Great Britain, but both had been born and trained in New Zealand.

Isabelle was tall and dark-haired, with a beautifully shaped, healthy-looking body, and of course a lovely face. The male lead was tall too, but his aquiline features and fine-boned, loose-limbed look contrasted with the rounded, animal vitality of his leading lady. As soon as they broke off a scene Isabelle would make straight for Greg, demanding a verdict on her performance, and Neville would saunter over to where Eloise sat

146

in an unobtrusive corner with a copy of the script and a pencil in hand.

In Thames two hotels had been booked for the cast and crew, and Eloise shared a room with the continuity girl. She managed to visit her parents several times, but most of the time she was on the set.

She and Greg were seldom alone, and no personal note intruded until one day, while the crew were packing up after the day's shooting, Greg called her to the caravan he was using as an office, and motioned her to sit down at the other side of the small folding table.

'Someone asked me today if we were back together,' he said.

'One of the crew?'

'No. A local guy who came to watch the filming.'

Among the extras recruited for the film, and the people who just came to watch, she had met a few she had previously known. 'Well,' she said slowly, 'it was bound to happen some time. What did you say?'

'Not much. Of course, the fact that we're married is going to spread. I'm surprised no one's picked it up already.'

'Perhaps it's common knowledge, and everyone's tactfully ignoring it.'

He was silent for a moment. 'Have you told Neville?'

'No.' The question had surprised her, and she didn't think before giving the bald answer. 'Have *you* told Isabelle?'

His brows drew together. 'No,' he said shortly. 'Why should I?'

'Why should I tell Neville?'

'You and he seem to be getting quite close.'

She blinked. Neville was good company and they spent some time talking together. It came naturally to him to try and charm any woman who crossed his path, but she knew he wasn't deeply involved, and certainly she wasn't. 'What about you and Isabelle?' she countered. Isabelle was forever tucking her hand in his arm or sitting with an arm casually draped on his shoulder.

His face went blank. 'What about us?'

'Aren't you—close?'

His expression didn't change, but his eyes narrowed fractionally. 'Would it matter to you if we were?'

'Would it matter to you if Neville and I were?'

For long moments they stared at each other, in a contest of wills. Then he got up abruptly, and took a stride away from her. In the tiny space, it brought him to the closed door. Swinging round to face her, he said, 'All right. Yes, it would. Now it's your turn.'

She opened her mouth to reply, when a knock came on the door.

Automatically, he swivelled his head, then looked at her again, waiting for an answer. His eyes held hers, demanding the truth, and she said quietly, 'Yes.'

He made to step towards her when there was another, louder knock.

He cursed under his breath, and threw open the door. 'Yes?' he said.

Isabelle said, 'Darling, help me up the step, will you?'

She climbed into the caravan, her hand still in his, her momentum carrying her forward, her free hand going to his chest and staying there. At first her concentration was all on Greg, then she caught sight of Eloise. 'Oh, sorry!' she said ruefully. 'I've interrupted your work.'

'Not at all,' said Eloise, rising quickly to her feet. 'I was just going.'

Greg said her name as she passed them, but Isabelle

was talking, about an end-of-shooting party. Eloise went down the steps and kept walking.

She had planned to go to bed early and to sleep late in the morning. But she felt restless and keyed up, and after dinner at the hotel, she decided to take a stroll.

She walked farther than she meant to, her thoughts chasing each other incoherently while she followed the foreshore and eventually drew away from the town environs, along the coast road that hugged steep cliffs on one side and skirted a series of rocky little bays on the other.

After some time she stopped, staring out over the silvered water to where the other coast of the gulf was still dimly visible. Greg had wanted to know if Neville and she were close. Greg was jealous.

Just supposing he did still love her? Where did that leave them? After the failures, the defections, of the past, and the final terrible brutality and then sheer downright callousness he had shown her, could they possibly put all that behind them and start afresh?

She didn't know. There had been faults on her side, too. She had been weak, timid, and worst of all she had not believed in him.

She was startled to discover that her watch read after ten-thirty. Shivering, she pulled her jacket about her as she turned to walk back to the town. By the time she reached the hotel, it was midnight.

After her long walk she should have slept like a log. Instead, she was troubled by disturbing dreams. The last one was extremely vivid. She dreamed that she saw Greg running through the bush, a pack of excited dogs yelping about him. A huge black boar with long, curved tusks suddenly appeared out of nowhere, and as the dogs rushed forward, it tossed them away one by one, goring them horribly with its tusks. Greg pulled out a knife from his belt and dived for its throat, but the boar first slashed his arm, making him drop the knife, then his legs, bringing him to the ground, and then it was on top of him, tearing and trampling, and making horrible grunting, snorting noises . . .

She tried to scream, but her throat was locked in sleep, and at last she woke up, sweating and terrified. Outside someone was starting a motorbike, and she looked at her watch in the first promise of daylight, to find it was almost five. The pig-hunters and the crew who were going out to film the hunt were to meet at five.

She lay gulping with relief. It was only a dream. Ever since the pig-hunt had been mentioned, stories had been floating round the set about past hunts. She had heard enough gory tales of dogs ripped up and stitched on the spot, hunters suffering nasty cuts and near misses, and boars as big as wild bulls and twice as nasty, to account for the terrifying realism of the dream. Greg would probably be nowhere near the actual hunt, but following the action from afar. If a pig did attack, there would be rifles as well as knives available to dispatch it long before it could do any real damage. The hunters prided themselves on doing the job with a knife, but if they could dispatch a pig without the risk of shooting one of their dogs, they would use a gun.

She looked at the other bed and saw her room-mate had left. She grabbed some clothes and rushed to the bathroom.

When she joined the group in the street around the Landcruisers which would carry the crew and equipment, Greg said, 'What are you doing here? There's no script for this take.'

Someone asked, 'Do we go with Tom?'

He said impatiently, 'Ask Debbie.' Debbie was his first assistant.

'I want to come,' Eloise said. 'Please!'

Most of the group were drifting away to the various vehicles. Neville, in a heavy grey woollen shirt, jeans and boots, with a soft hat, put a friendly arm about Eloise's shoulders. 'Hello,' he said. 'Are you going to come and see me take my life in my hands?'

Someone called, 'Greg? Are we all set?'

'Yes,' he said, half-turning, then directed an inimical look at Eloise. 'All right. But don't get in the way.'

Neville smiled down at Eloise. 'You can sit next to me.'

The journey into the bush was over a rough, unsealed road, ending in a mile of clay track that was grassy and pot-holed. The tall trees and delicate fronded ferns were dewy and the rising sun set them shimmering. The convoy halted at the top of a rise where the clay road abruptly stopped at the edge of the bush, and in the sudden silence bird calls echoed from tree to tree with a startling clarity.

The hunters, who had led the way in an ancient truck, began collecting their gear and letting loose the dogs that had been tied on the tray. Lean and scarred, the animals milled about, panting and excited.

One of the hunters, dressed in a torn tartan shirt, thick baggy trousers and boots caked with old mud, sniffed the air and said, 'Dry as a bone. Pigs'll be down the gullies.'

His companion gathered the dogs with a series of whistles and commands. The crew unloaded tripods, lights, cameras and microphones while the assistant director and the 'grip' supervised. The continuity girl snapped the two hunters with an instant camera, and they clowned, posing exaggeratedly. Neville wandered over at the continuity girl's call, to check his costume against his double. Eloise leaned against the bonnet of the dusty vehicle she had travelled in, glad of the respite. The trip over rough roads had made her feel queasy. Bevan, the actor who was playing the other hunter, lounged beside her.

Greg came over to them, holding a clipboard, and said to Bevan, 'Go and get yourself checked for continuity.' Then to Eloise he said softly, 'Where were you last night?'

'I—went for a walk.'

'Until midnight?'

'Yes. About that.' She hesitated. 'Did you want me?'

His mouth hardened. 'You could say that.'

He seemed about to say something more, but Neville returned then, and said cheerfully, 'What sort of derring-do are you planning for me, Greg?'

'None,' Greg said crisply. 'We can't risk your neck, it's too precious. The hunters will find you a place that's close to where we hope the action will be, without being dangerous. The cameras will try to get some action shots of the chase, and Stanley will take his mikes as close as he can. After we've filmed the real thing, we'll get you and Bevan to run over the ground. Then we'll try a few fakes with a dead pig, if we get one. Till then, you just keep out of the way.'

Neville looked at Eloise. 'That makes two of us. Well, I dare say we can pass the time well enough.'

'With the rest of the crew who aren't immediately needed,' Greg said.

Neville grinned. 'Spoilsport.'

The hunters set a cracking pace, but in twenty

minutes they had reached a knoll that looked over several deep gullies. Greg surveyed the terrain and conferred with the hunters. One of them handed him a rifle.

Eloise said, 'What are you going to do?' Her dream came back in vivid detail, and she couldn't help a shiver of apprehension.

'Cover the cameraman,' he said. 'Just in case something goes wrong.'

The hunters and their dogs skirted one of the gullies, every now and then lost to sight among the scrubby trees and wild gorse. One cameraman and the focus puller who would adjust the camera for him stopped on a spot on a ridge. The other, with a cumbersome hired 'Steadicam' harnessed to his shoulder, was following behind the hunters, and Greg stayed between them, while the sound man dodged from bush to bush.

On the knoll the little group of people who would be needed for the faked shots afterwards waited patiently with their equipment.

One of the dogs barked and plunged into the gully, the others trailing behind. The hunters quickened their pace, and there was a shaking of bushes as some large animal made its way along the floor of the gully.

The dogs were visible in quick glimpses of white or brown or brindle, and the hunters were running now, following the dogs.

Then the dogs broke into excited barks, and there was a loud squealing. A patch of dense bush in the gully shivered madly, and a dull black shape, long and solid and snorting indignantly, shot from the gully over the ridge and into the next hollow, with two dogs at its heels.

The men pounded over the ridge and disappeared after the animals. Greg, trying to stay out of camera range, signalled the first camera closer, and scrambled up a small rise to try and get a better view.

The next time the pig appeared, a dog was hanging on to its tail, but the boar shook it off and circled back as the other dogs appeared to cut off its line of retreat.

It galloped across a clearing and hurled itself into the cover of the bush again, crashing through the manuka scrub, coming towards the knoll from which Eloise and the others were watching.

'Someone told me they always run downhill,' Neville said nervously.

The mobile cameraman wheeled and went after the hunters. Greg broke into a run, too, dodging and weaving among the trees, closing in along with the others, but keeping behind the camera.

For a while the watchers could see nothing except swaying bushes and occasional flashes of colour—the red and black of a tartan shirt, the flag of a dog's tail. Then a terrible commotion broke out—squealing, snorting, barks, snarls, and the shouts and whistles of the men.

Eloise turned away, putting her hands over her ears. But she heard Neville's excited voice moments later saying, 'He's away again!'

She dropped her hands, and looked. A hunter swore so loudly that the words floated clearly up to the knoll, and the men laughed. But Eloise was staring down at what was happening in the gully.

Greg was still standing in the same place, his head cocked in a listening attitude. The man in front of him was assiduously filming, and Eloise saw Greg glance towards the other cinematographer and the sound man to make sure they were safe. But down at that level he couldn't see what she could from her vantage point—the ominous swaying of the bushes as the boar cut a path through them, cunningly turning again in a circle away from its pursuers, and heading straight for where Greg stood.

She shrieked, '*Greg!*' And as he looked up, the boar broke cover and streaked across the space, ears bloody and torn from the dogs, its mouth gaping open and two curved, yellowed tusks ready for attack.

Greg was standing quite still, but Eloise began to run, hurling herself down the hill faster than she had ever run in her life, reaching the bottom in seconds, and the boar, distracted by the movement, finding her between him and his escape route, charged.

Eloise, still running, tried to change direction in mid-flight, somehow twisted her knee and fell heavily on her back. She heard shouting, and a loud, hoarse grunting, horribly near, and screamed as the boar reached her.

The world became a blur of blood and hard, bruising hooves and razor sharp tusks, terrifyingly close to her face, and the weight and stench of a hundred pounds of flesh and bone and muscle, covered in coarse black hair. Instinctively she flung up her arms to protect her face. There was a deafening noise, followed by another. The dogs were barking, the men yelling, then the frightening, ghastly weight was dragged off as she heard Greg's voice, and then saw his face, white and furious, hovering over her. '*You bloody little fool! What the hell are you doing?*'

CHAPTER TWELVE

'I'M sorry,' Eloise said shakily. 'I've ruined your take, haven't I?'

Greg cast her a look of total exasperation and said, 'If you weren't hurt, I'd shake the daylights out of you!' Then he shouted to someone, 'Where's the first aid box? Will you *bring* it, for God's sake?'

They bandaged her knee and a small gash on her arm where the boar's tusk had gone through her sweater and shirt before Greg's shot had killed it. Then Greg and one of the other men made a chair of their hands and carried her to the vehicles. 'I'll just sit here,' she said, 'until you finish filming.'

'Shut up!' Greg snarled. 'I've had enough of your stupidity for one day!'

He drove her to the hospital himself, leaving the others to finish the scene under the first assistant's supervision, and crowd into the remaining vehicles for the homeward trip as best they could. Once there he sat and waited until the doctor and nurses had put stitches in the wound and X-rayed the knee and her sore ribs, to find no great damage.

'I'll take you to your parents' place,' he said.

'Thank you,' she said meekly. 'That's very thoughtful.'

On the way he suddenly said, 'I shouldn't have let you come in the first place. Why on earth did you want to, anyway?'

They had given her an injection of antibiotic and then some pain reliever. She felt light and uncaring, rather floaty. 'I had a dream,' she said, 'that the boar attacked *you*.'

He looked incredulous. After a moment he said, 'You were trying to *protect* me?' Then, 'For God's sake, woman! *I* was the one with the gun!'

'I know,' she said. 'But I didn't think. I just saw him coming towards you and——' her voice wobbled and she said resentfully, '—and you've been snapping and snarling at me ever since. I've told you I'm *sorry* I ruined your filming, but you didn't have to——'

He swore and pulled over to the side of the road. Hauling her into his arms, he said roughly, 'The hell with the filming! I didn't mean to snarl—only you gave me such a damned fright!'

His mouth descended on hers, the kiss was a strange blend of passion, frustration and release, but after a little while his mouth softened and it became light and sweet and comforting. Releasing her, he said, 'You're as pale as death. I'd better get you home to bed.'

Her mother first flew at Greg as though it was all his fault, and then fussed Eloise into bed in five minutes from the time of their arrival. She was drifting into sleep when Greg came in. 'I'm going to my hotel to get some things,' he said. 'I'll be back. I'm in the spare room.'

'There's no need,' she said. 'You have so much to do—the film——'

'I don't need the coals of fire, thanks,'

'What?' she said drowsily.

'Never mind.' He bent to kiss her lips, hard and quickly.

When she woke it was nearly morning, and he was straddling a chair by her bed, his arms resting on its back.

'Have you been there all night?' she asked wonderingly.

'I couldn't sleep, anyway. Can I get you anything?'

'No——' Then, changing her mind, 'Perhaps some lemonade.'

Her mother appeared in the doorway, saying, 'Is anything wrong? Did you want something, Eloise?'

'I was going to look for some lemonade,' Greg told her.

'I'll get it.'

When she had gone, Eloise said, 'What did you mean—coals of fire?'

'First you throw yourself in front of a raging wild boar in some misguided effort to "save" me, then you keep bravely saying, "Leave me".' He paused. 'But you don't really want me to leave, do you?'

She looked away from him, and he said, his voice shaking with the effort to keep it level, 'Dammit, Eloise, I know what I did to you was unforgivable, but you *love* me! It has to make *some* difference!'

Her mother returned just then, a glass in her hand, and switched on the light. Greg cast his eyes heavenwards. Eloise wanted to giggle.

She made to sit up, and Greg clumsily arranged the pillow behind her. Throwing him a glance of near-contempt, her mother put the glass on the bedside table while she made a better job of it. Then she handed Eloise the glass and watched while she drank half the lemonade and replaced the glass on the table.

'I need the bathroom.' Pushing away the covers, Eloise tried to stand, but her leg had stiffened overnight, and she gasped with pain and abruptly sat down again. Her mother darted forward. 'I'll help you.'

But Greg stepped determinedly in front of her, scooping Eloise easily into his arms. 'My department, I think, Mrs Dalton,' he said.

Her mother moved out of the way, her lips compressed, and Eloise, her patience suddenly snapping, said, 'Oh, for heaven's sake, you two! You're like a couple of dogs with a bone. Greg has a *right* to be here and to help me, Mum, he's my husband! I'm an adult now, not your baby girl. What's more, it isn't up to you to decide what—or who—is good for me. And Greg,' she said, turning her face up to him, 'it's stupid and childish and utterly ridiculous for you to be jealous of my *mother*! You've never seen that I can love anyone else without detracting from my love for you. I suppose because you had no family of your own, you can't see that love isn't like that—it has no limits, it just stretches to accommodate more people all the time, and it doesn't become thinner in the process, only deeper and richer ... oh, take me to the bathroom!' she finished crossly. 'I've made my speech, and I don't suppose either of you will listen.'

Some minutes later, Greg entered the kitchen where Mrs Dalton was boiling the kettle and spooning tea into a teapot. She looked up, and for a moment he hesitated in the doorway, looking back at her. 'She's having a bath,' he said. 'She said she'll call when she needs help.'

'Would you like a cup of tea?' Mrs Dalton asked stiffly.

'Thanks. Can I help?'

'No, it's nearly done. Sit down. Do you want toast?'

'Not now.' He took a chair at the table in the centre of the big room, sitting with his hands in front of him, curled into fists. She put a cup before him, and sat down herself. Spooning sugar into her tea, she said, 'I didn't mean that yesterday—when you brought her home. I just got a bit of a shock, you know.'

He looked up, then. 'I know. She told me I did nothing but snap and snarl at her from the moment it happened. That was shock, too.'

Mrs Dalton nodded. She said, 'When she was three, and we were shopping in town, she ran into the road. A truck just missed her. I screamed, and when she ran back to me I picked her up and spanked her, right in front of everyone in the street, and called her a stupid girl.'

'I understand the feeling. I might have spanked her myself, yesterday, if she'd been up to it.'

'Well,' she said, 'she's too big for me to do it, any more.' Ruefully, Greg laughed, and she laughed a little, too. 'Not that I believe in wife-beating,' she added warningly.

'It's all right. Neither do I.'

A strangely doubtful expression flitted across her face.

A line of colour lay along Greg's cheekbones. He said, 'Did she tell you what happened—before I went to America?'

Mrs Dalton shook her head. 'I know something did— but I could only guess. She wouldn't talk about it. But she was terribly upset.' Remembered anger lit her eyes for a moment, followed by surprise as Greg winced. She took a deep breath and said, 'But that's between you and her. You don't have to tell me.'

He said, 'I'd rather not. Chiefly because I'm ashamed of it.' He paused, looking down at his cup. 'She's probably right, about me being jealous. I do find it hard—to share. I'm not used to it.'

'She was probably right about a lot of things. Drink your tea—it'll get cold.'

When Eloise called, Mrs Dalton said, 'Well, go on. She needs you.'

Eloise spent the day lying on the sofa in the lounge, after firmly sending Greg back to the film set. 'And don't tell me I'm being a martyr again,' she said. 'It's my film, too, remember. I'll probably be back on the set myself by tomorrow.'

He left reluctantly, promising to return as soon as shooting finished for the day.

'He's worried about you,' her mother told her.

'He needn't be. I got off lightly, considering.'

'You still love him, don't you?'

'Yes,' Eloise said. 'I still do.'

'Well ...' Her mother sighed. 'If that's what you want.'

He brought her flowers, and a box of chocolates from the crew.

'They're all concerned about you,' he said. 'Neville wants to visit you. I told him, after dinner.'

'That will be nice.'

He shot her a look, then said, 'Were you with him, the other night?'

Eloise looked blank, and he said impatiently, 'The night before the pig-hunt. We got interrupted in the caravan, and when I came looking for you later, you weren't in the hotel. I waited for hours. No one said, but I could tell they thought you were together. Were you?'

She shook her head. 'I have no idea where Neville was. I went for a walk. I was thinking, and I walked further than I realised.'

He had his hands in his pockets. 'That's why I let you come,' he said. 'I had some crazy idea we'd get a chance to talk. Instead——' he indicated her injuries, '—this happened.'

'It doesn't matter. It was my own fault—as you pointed out.'

Greg came to sit on the sofa beside her, taking her hand in a hard clasp. 'You darling idiot! What on earth did you think you could do?'

'I don't know. I wasn't really thinking at all.'

'I did wonder if you were coming along to be with Neville, but ...'

He bent towards her, and she smiled into his eyes. Mrs Dalton appeared in the doorway, muttered. 'Oh, excuse me!' and made to retreat.

Greg straightened up, still holding Eloise by the hand, and turned his head. 'It's all right,' he said formally. 'Come in.'

She hesitated. 'I thought you might like a cup of tea. Dinner will be another hour or so. And what about you, Eloise?'

Eloise accepted, and Greg said, 'Thank you, Mrs Dalton, that would be very welcome. Are you having one? Shall we drink ours with Eloise?'

She looked startled, but Eloise said quickly, 'That would be nice.'

Her mother caught sight of the flowers. 'From you, Greg?'

He nodded.

'I'll put them in water,' she offered, and bore them away.

'The other night,' Greg said, 'if you'd said Neville was important to you, I was all ready for the big renunciation scene. If he's the one you want ... I won't stand in your way, etcetera.'

'May the best man win?'

He nodded. 'You struck home with that remark about real love being generous. I don't know if I could have gone through with it, but I'd psyched myself up to trying, anyway.'

Eloise said softly, 'You fool!'

A threatening glint appeared in his eyes, and she said hurriedly, deciding attack was the best means of defence, 'What about Isabelle?'

'Beautiful and talented and intelligent—and a pest.' Eloise looked at him quizzically.

'Well, all right,' he conceded. 'I enjoyed her attention, mainly because it helped my bruised ego. And I did hope that it might bother you if I played up to her. But that night when she came barging in, I could have strangled the woman. I got rid of her and came after you, but you'd taken off. I was afraid that you'd decided I was stringing you along and gone off to console yourself with Neville.'

'I would never have done that. Any more than I——'

There was a heartbeat's silence. 'I know,' said Greg in a low voice. 'You never have. I've known for a long time I was wrong ... I think I knew it even then.'

'It was so—crazy.'

'Yes, I guess I *was* a little crazy that day. Although that's no excuse. I suppose I'd built this scenario up in my head, I'd been planning it for such a long time. And then nothing went according to plan ... somebody threw away the script and I didn't know how to do the scene any more.'

He had driven down to the farm from Auckland, not in a borrowed farm vehicle this time, but in a sleek new continental car that had cost him an arm and a leg and then some. And instead of a bush shirt and jeans he wore designer slacks and an expensive imported shirt. He knew he looked the picture of success, and was deliberately flaunting it. He wasn't in fact as affluent as the carefully cultivated image suggested. But he was on his way, and knew it. He was going to saunter into the Dalton household, show Eloise's parents that they had been absolutely wrong about him, and whisk her away from right under their noses, dazzled and eager to accompany him while he conquered fresh fields overseas.

Over the past couple of years the overwhelming bitterness and pain of her desertion had been subjugated by hard, stimulating work. All his energy had gone into making a success of the film company, fulfilling the promises that Basil Blakeney had made. Without conceit, he knew it was largely due to his energy and drive and his faith in his own ability that their first film had brought together a team of fine actors and excellent technicians, all contributing to the polished product that impressed both the critics and the public, and received an honourable mention at Cannes. From there they had moved to greater heights with relative ease. Everyone wanted to work with Greg Stone, and he could pick and choose his team to his own satisfaction.

After that first triumph he had been tempted to confront Eloise and her parents then and there, but instead, conscious that one good film didn't make a career, he had forced himself to wait, hardly taking a breath between his first venture and the next, consolidating his reputation until no one could have called his earlier work a flash in the pan. Already he was known for working fast and hard, exhausting everyone else on the set, but getting his film into the can in record time. The latest was barely out, but it had premièred in London and New York, and word was spreading like wildfire: *Stone has done it again.* Even the British and American critics were taking notice. There was talk of the New Zealand film industry finding its feet, of a fresh antipodean vision.

And now he was at a turning point. This was the moment to bring the dead dragon to the feet of the princess, and claim her for his own. He was tense with anticipation, his palms slipping on the steering wheel

just at the thought of seeing her again, his mind filled
with images of her, his body going hot and cold and hot
again, remembering the silkiness of her hair, the smooth
sheen of her skin, the way she laughed with her head to
one side, the cool touch of her hand in his, her mouth
moving under his lips ...

And at last, confronted with the unexpected, the
anticipation, the tension, had turned in on itself and
boiled over into disaster and ugliness ...

Eloise, too, remembered that day vividly. Her parents
had gone to the wedding of a cousin living in Rotorua,
and she had been planning to wash the sheets and some
clothes, only to find the washing machine had broken
down. A repair man came out and fixed it, but by the
time he had finished it was afternoon. While hanging the
clean clothes on the line she heard a persistent bellowing
and, following the sound over a hill near the house,
discovered one of the young beef cattle lying on the
ground with a grotesquely swollen stomach.

She recognised the symptoms of bloat, and her heart
sank. Knowing her father had drench for the condition,
she ran back to the farm buildings and spent ten minutes
finding it and making up a dose. Then she hunted for a
knife, praying she would not have to use it, and raced
back to the paddock and the stricken animal.

Getting the drench down its throat was a nightmare of
frustration. The half-grown bullock rolled its eyes and
struggled and spilled a good deal of the stuff, along with
its own grass-tinted saliva, down the front of her dress.
She looked up with vast relief when a male voice said,
'Trouble, Ell? Can I help?'

'Oh, I wish you would, Craig. My father's away, and I
haven't done this before.' Never had a neighbour been so
welcome.

'Saw you from my place, so I nipped over the fence. Reckon he's too far gone for drench,' Craig grunted. 'Got a knife?'

She handed it to him and flinched as he plunged it into the swollen stomach of the beast in just the right place to release the gas which would have killed it.

Half an hour later the animal was on its feet, grazing as though nothing had happened. Craig came back to the house and rang the vet for her, asking him to check the bullock next day, while she showered and changed and then made a pot of tea.

Craig was young, single and good-looking. He had been share-milking in the district for some years and had only recently bought the adjoining dairy farm. Once or twice he had made overtures in Eloise's direction which she had firmly turned off, and he bore no grudge. She guessed he could just about take his pick of girls anyway, and one day soon he would make his choice and settle down to a life of domesticated bliss.

She saw him out to the door, and as they stood on the top step of the veranda, said, 'I don't know how to thank you.'

He looked at her teasingly. 'Don't you? I'll show you, then.'

She didn't resist as he grasped her shoulders and bent to kiss her mouth, but when he would have pulled her closer, his lips firming on hers, she put her hands on his chest and pushed him gently away.

'Well,' he said, smiling down at her, 'you can't blame a bloke for trying. You're not offended, are you?'

'No. But you know I don't——'

'I should know by now,' he said ruefully. 'You're not interested.'

They turned together as the car drew up before the steps, the engine so quiet it had been almost there before they noticed it. 'Someone you know?' asked Craig as Greg stepped out and slammed the door.

Stunned, Eloise nodded, and Craig said, 'I'll be off, then.'

He nodded to Greg, giving him a curious glance as he passed, and receiving only a glacial stare in return. Greg leaned back against the car with his arms folded until Craig had disappeared from sight.

Eloise found her voice. 'What are you doing here?'

Unfolding his arms, Greg came slowly up the steps. 'I came to see you.' He reached the second step, bringing his eyes level with hers. 'And who's the gentleman caller?'

'Just a neighbour.'

'Oh,' he said sarcastically. 'Is that all?'

'Yes. That's all.' She supposed he had seen the kiss, but in this mood she didn't think he deserved an explanation. Of course, she thought resignedly, the first time a man had touched her in two years would have to be just when he happened along. Life, as Somerset Maugham once said, was a bad joke written in poor taste. 'Do you want to come in?' she asked him, swinging about to re-enter the house, leaving him to follow.

He did so without speaking, and in the lounge he looked at the two teacups and said, 'Where are your parents?'

'Out.' She picked up the cups and saucers. 'Do you want some tea?'

'No, thanks. It must have been cosy, just you and your—neighbour.'

She stood for a moment with the crockery in her hands and looked straight at him. Then without speaking she took the things through to the kitchen, depositing them in the sink before returning to the lounge.

He was standing where she had left him, his hands jammed in his pockets, looking somehow threatening.

'Why have you come?' she asked.

'I've brought some money for you.'

'I don't want your money.'

'Not mine. Yours. It's to pay back the amount you invested in the company, with interest added at the going rate.'

'That was *your* savings.'

'Ours. We were living on your wages at the time. I couldn't have saved any money, otherwise.' He took a folded cheque from his pocket and held it out to her.

'I told you I don't want it.'

'Take it. I don't want to be owing you anything!' he said.

She wondered what he meant. After two years' separation, divorce was relatively simple. She had never allowed herself to think that far ahead, turning off her mother's enquiries into what she intended to do about her broken marriage, living from day to day.

'Take it,' he repeated harshly.

Eloise stretched out her hand and took the cheque from him, standing with it folded in her fingers.

She looked cool and indifferent, and he was burning with suppressed rage and desire, inwardly castigating himself for not even considering the possibility that she might have found someone else. The princess was supposed to remain in her ivory tower, safely out of reach of other men, until the dragon was slain.

Maybe the neighbour was no one special, the kiss had not been prolonged, but seeing them together had jolted him badly, forcing him to consider new possibilities— frightening ones. 'You're very friendly with your neighbours,' he said, not intending to say it at all, certainly not meaning to inject that jeering note into his voice.

Her head went up. 'Craig is a friend, yes.'

'Do you always kiss him goodbye?'

At least that got a reaction—a spark of anger in her eyes, a slight compression of her lips before she answered, 'No, not always.'

That meant *sometimes*, didn't it? He took a step towards her, looking goaded and dangerous. '*I* might have expected a kiss when I arrived,' he said. 'You know, a wifely greeting after two years apart.'

Her eyes widened a little, and her lips parted, not with anticipation, he saw, but with indignation, perhaps tinged with fear. A small ripple of mean satisfaction ran through him, but his gaze was riveted on her mouth, and in two strides he had covered the distance between them and jerked her into his arms.

If she had yielded even a little, he might have managed to be gentle, but her body was rigidly resistant, her hands straining against him, only her mouth soft and helpless under his as she tried to get away from him. Determined to force a response from her, he placed a compelling hand at her nape, holding her still as his mouth hardened, then his other hand found her breast, and his raging desire became white-hot.

When she managed to wrench herself free, and her hand swung back and delivered a stinging blow to his cheek, he hardly felt it. With her hair dishevelled by his handling, her burning cheeks making her eyes brilliant, her mouth moistly pink and swollen from the violence of his kiss, she looked blindingly beautiful, and he could only stare at her with furious passion naked in his eyes.

She said chokingly, 'If you've finished, will you please go!'

He tried to leash his emotions, to keep his voice steady.

'I haven't finished,' he said. That sounded flat, colourless. Better than yelling, he supposed. 'I have a proposition for you.'

She didn't speak, and he shoved his hands into his pockets to stop himself from hauling her back into his arms, and turned away. 'I'm going to America,' he said, and because he wasn't looking at her he missed the startled anguish that flashed across her face. 'I've been invited to make films in Hollywood, for one of the big studios. All facilities provided, no expense spared more or less, more money than I could dream of here.'

She said huskily, 'Congratulations.'

He swung to face her then. Was she being sarcastic? He couldn't tell, because her face was blank and smooth, the angry colour fading from her cheeks, leaving them oddly white. His own barely contained anger stirred again. Was that all she had to say? Would she have let him go without a word, without a hint of protest or regret?

He said, 'Even your parents will admit that I'm able to keep you now, in the style to which they would like you to be accustomed. I'm a better bet than anyone you'll find around here, Eloise—including your friendly neighbouring farmer.'

She said, 'What do you mean?'

What sort of game was she playing with him? How could she not know what he meant? He could hardly keep his hands off her, couldn't stop his eyes from wandering over her body, knowing she must see the wanting in them. Did he have to spell it out for her?

'You'd go well in Hollywood,' he said. 'An asset to any man. I can give you everything you ever wanted. It would mean leaving your family, of course, but surely at twenty-two you can live without being tied to your mother's apron strings? And I'd make sure there'd be plenty of compensations. A beautiful home, plenty of money—a husband you don't need to be ashamed of—it's all yours for the asking. Clothes, of course—you ought to have clothes that do justice to your looks.'

'You're asking me to go with you?'

He thought, *of course I'm damn well asking you*! What did she want him to do? Beg? Go on his knees? Frustrated by her lack of reaction, and increasingly, miserably angry, he said, trying to sound indifferent to her answer for his pride's sake, 'You're my wife—you're entitled to first refusal. So—how about it?'

She was staring at him, with an expression he couldn't fathom, the pupils of her eyes expanded enormously, so that her green eyes looked dark in a white face.

'No,' she said. 'No, thank you!'

No? His fantasy shattered with a word, Greg mentally reeled under the unexpected refusal. He had been so sure that even though she had allowed her parents' conventional views to prevail, even though she had defected from their marriage and run back home, the love they had shared so stormily could not have died. They could damp it down as much as they liked, but the embers would always be there, ready to burst into a wild, consuming flame. He had only to touch her for the spark to kindle into life. And he knew, he *knew* it had been the same for her. No matter how far apart they were, or for how long, he had not believed for a moment that they could lose that, that either one of them could exist for ever without the other. He had forced himself to be patient, to exercise superhuman will-power, but it had only been possible because of that deep-held unshakeable conviction that ultimately he must win her back to him. And whatever it took, that he would do.

And yet, minutes ago, she had been ice in his arms, rejection in every bone and sinew of her body. And now she was turning him down, throwing his offerings, his triumphs, his two years of self-discipline, the proof that on her own terms he was worthy of her love, back at him as though it wasn't worth a snap of her fingers.

Resentfully, he said, 'Most women would jump at the chance——'

'Oh, I'm sure they would. Why don't you ask one of them? I'm flattered to be first on the list, but I'm sure you'll have no trouble——'

'*Damn* you, Eloise!' he snapped, his anger breaking the hold he had on it. 'You're my *wife*, I'm leaving the country, and I want to take you with me.'

'I'm not your possession,' she said clearly. 'And I wouldn't go with you to the end of the street.' One closed hand opened, and she threw his crumpled cheque down at his feet.

He realised that she was almost as angry as he. It seemed totally unreasonable. Everything had gone wrong, and he couldn't figure out how to make it right again. His mind suddenly presented him with a clear, taunting picture of Eloise locked in another man's arms, as she had been when he arrived. His confidence in their future wavered in a rising panic. The ugly suspicion that he had been repressing ever since he had seen her with Craig came spilling to the surface of his mind, and jealousy—violent, uncontrollable, destructive— brought a horrid, metallic taste to his mouth and made his hands tremble and his jaw go tight. A haze of red and black spots obscured his vision, and he narrowed his eyes against it, focusing on her face.

'You've found someone else?' he said nastily. 'What a fool I am. I don't know why I thought that while you were married to me, you would be at least physically faithful.'

Even as he said it, he expected—or at least hoped for—

a denial. She didn't deny it, she just stared at him, her eyes quite blank and expressionless. Deliberately so, he thought, hiding her thoughts, hiding her—guilt?

The blood rushed into his temples, making them throb. Sweat beaded his brow. He *had* been a fool. She wasn't denying it because obviously she couldn't. One thing Eloise had never been was a liar. He gave a small, bitter laugh. What an idiot, he thought. Weaving his foolish daydreams while she played around with other men.

At last she said, her voice scarcely more than a whisper, 'I think—you'd better go.'

'Sure,' he said. What else was there to do? The whole exercise had been a disaster from start to finish. He made to walk to the door, and she stood aside hastily, as though an accidental touch might contaminate her. He stopped and looked at her, and his hands ached for the feel of her skin under his fingertips, the small weight of her breast in his palm. He said, 'I might not see you again for a long time. You can at least kiss me goodbye.'

Even as he reached for her, he despised himself for making the excuse. The truth was he couldn't keep his hands off her, and he had an overpowering longing to have her close to him, her lips against his, just this once more, even for a moment.

But his grip, in the stress of his feelings, was painful, and she instinctively pulled back, trying to avoid his mouth. And that was when the anger and frustration and torment burst all the bonds he had imposed on them. His teeth clenched, and he said, 'You're still married to me, and I have a right to more than a kiss.' Then he reached for her again, and this time there was no chance of escape. 'If you can give yourself to other men, you can damn well do the same for me.' His kiss was savage, his hands on her body rough and uncaring. He used no more force than was necessary to stop her hurting him or getting away from his increasingly callous caresses, but there was no doubt in either of their minds that his intention was punishment, humiliation, revenge.

'I'll never forgive you for this, Greg. *Never!*'

CHAPTER THIRTEEN

NEVILLE, arriving with an armload of flowers, soon had Stan chuckling at a joke, and without exerting himself at all, charmed Mrs Dalton completely. When he had left, kissing Eloise on her cheek and promising to procure for her anything she cared to express a wish for, Greg said, 'I shouldn't have let that fellow come.'

Eloise's smile was strained.

'You're tired,' he said. 'I'll carry you to bed.'

'I'd rather walk,' she said a little sharply. 'If you'll just help.'

Her mother helped her into her nightgown, and when she was in bed, Greg came back and asked, 'Is there anything else you want?'

Eloise shook her head.

'Goodnight, then.' He bent over her, hesitating for a fraction of a second with his lips poised above hers before he deflected his kiss to her cheek, because she hadn't offered the slightest hint of response.

Her mother asked, 'Would you like a hot drink, to help you sleep?'

She smiled. 'Well, all right.'

Mrs Dalton disappeared in the direction of the kitchen and Greg, looking thoughtfully at Eloise, took her hand. 'I wish you'd stop putting up those fences,' he said quietly. 'I've said it more than once—I was a monster and a heel. I could apologise a hundred times over, but it can't undo what I did to you. I know that. I know you're not ever going to forget it, because you can't—any more than I can. But holding it against me is making *you* unhappy. That's what I can't stand.'

'I can't help it.' The hurt he had inflicted had been deep. The fact that he had forced her was bad enough, but it was the later betrayal that had irrevocably wounded her. That was when she had told herself she must finally accept that whatever he felt for her, it was not love.

She said, 'Give me time.'

And Greg, his mouth wry, asked, 'How much more time do you need, Eloise? I seem to have been waiting all my life for you. Waiting for you to grow up—waiting until I could give you what I thought you wanted, needed. How long do I have to wait for you to forgive me?'

'Is it too much to ask?'

Her lingering bitterness showed, and she saw how he checked himself before he said evenly, 'If it takes for ever, it's not too much to ask. I'll stand any amount of punishment, if that's what you want. But I know you too well to imagine that would make you happy. And your happiness is what *I* want, above all else. Maybe it's arrogant of me to think I can give you that. But you can't deny that you've given me good reason to hope . . .'

Her mother arrived with a cup of Milo, and although he didn't let it pass, Eloise noticed that Greg's humorous grimace was almost tolerant.

They made some slightly stilted conversation while she drank it, and then Greg removed the cup and straightened her pillow. 'Anything else?'

She shook her head. 'No, thank you.'

He smiled. 'And if you want anything tomorrow,' he said, with a glint in his eye, 'ask *me*, not Neville.'

Mrs Dalton took the cup from him. 'I'll fix that. Goodnight, dear.'

'Goodnight. You've both been so good. Thanks for looking after me.'

'Mothers are meant for that,' said Mrs Dalton lightly.

'And husbands,' Greg added. 'In sickness and in health . . .'

Mrs Dalton said, 'It's a pity you didn't remember that last time.'

Eloise said sharply, *'Mum!'*

Greg's attention was arrested. 'Last time?' he said blankly.

Eloise moved, frantically trying to attract her mother's eye, but her gaze was fixed on Greg, both of them apparently oblivious. 'When she had the car accident,' Mrs Dalton said clearly. 'And lost the baby.'

Eloise made a small sound of protest, but the other two were still staring at each other. The colour drained from Greg's face. It was moments before he spoke, and when he did, his voice sounded strange. 'What car accident?' he demanded hoarsely. *'What baby?'*

Eloise closed her eyes. She heard her mother say, 'She hasn't told you?' And then, 'You'd better ask Eloise.' When her mother had quietly closed the door Greg was still standing there beside the bed. He said, 'Eloise? Eloise, for God's sake open your eyes.' And then he repeated, 'What car accident? What baby?'

'It was yours,' she said swiftly, defensively.

He flinched. 'Yes. When?' His throat was constricted, he had difficulty forcing the words past it.

'After you went overseas.'

He said slowly, 'Then it could only have been conceived when——'

'Yes,' Eloise confirmed.

'My God,' he said quietly, tearingly. 'How you must have hated me!'

'I thought I did,' she confessed. 'For a long time.' But as the baby grew inside her she had known it was a part of Greg too, and she couldn't help loving the baby. 'I centred all my attention on the baby. I tried not to think of anything else, and after a while, when I did think of you it was with a sort of merciful blankness.'

His jaw clenched at that, but he didn't speak.

'When I was six months pregnant, I was in a car accident, driving to Auckland with a friend. She was quite badly injured, in hospital for months. I was lucky, I suppose, nothing but a broken arm and a few bruises. Except that I went into premature labour . . . and the baby died.'

Greg was standing very still, his eyes almost painfully fixed on her. She went on, her voice low, her hands suddenly clenching convulsively on the coverlet in front of her. 'They tried to stop her being born so soon . . . for a while they were quite hopeful . . . the whole thing took a few days. That was when we sent the cable.'

'Cable?'

'The cable to you,' she said with a hint of impatience. 'I was in pain and frightened and I knew our baby was being born and might die before you could even see her. Somehow the hatred had all gone away, and I only knew that I needed you. What you believed about my motives didn't matter, and the fact that I had hurt you terribly, and you had been brutal to me, didn't seem to matter so much, either. Dad got an address from Basil Blakeney. My mother wanted to tell you what had happened, but I thought if you knew what was wrong you might come out of guilt, a sense of responsibility . . . so I told them what the cable should say.'

'What did it say?'

She looked at him with anger. 'You don't remember?'

'I don't know what it said. Tell me.'

'Just *Please come. I need you.* If you loved me, you would have . . .'

'Yes,' he said, 'I would have. I never got any cable.'

She was stunned. In all the time while anticipation had turned to doubt, and doubt to despair and finally, at last, to what she had thought was pure, bitter hatred, this possibility had never occurred to her.

'How could you not have got it?' she demanded. What cruel trick of fate could have led that particular cable to go astray?

'I don't know,' he said. 'But I swear I never got it. Who sent it?'

'My mother.'

His face changed slowly. She could see a pulse beat in his temple, his eyes had gone unfocused and his mouth turned down. His fists clenched, until he turned to the dressing-table and brought them down on its surface. '*The bitch!*' he said. 'She never bloody sent it!'

'She did!' Eloise cried. 'Of course she did!'

'How do you know?' he shouted. 'She's always loathed me. It must have seemed a golden opportunity to make sure you never wanted to contact me again. She knew you couldn't forgive *that*!'

'Greg, it isn't true! It *isn't*!'

Again he said, enunciating every word, his eyes boring into hers, 'How do you know?'

She stared back at him, and finally said quietly, 'Greg, I *know*. I know the same way I know you never received it. You wouldn't lie about it—and neither would she. I believe you—and I believe her.'

Gradually the fury left his face, to be replaced by acceptance. 'All right,' he said finally. 'All right.' He shook his head, and passed a hand over his hair. 'If I had known——' he muttered. 'You don't know what hell I went through, those first few months. I kept thinking I'd contact you ... phone ... fly back here ... ask you again to forgive me, but then I thought, how could you ... how could any woman forgive something like that? I wrote a lot of abject letters that got torn up.'

'It doesn't matter now,' she said. 'I know I said I'd never forgive you—and it took time, but that was easy compared with the other.'

She was suddenly very tired. Her eyelids drooped. She felt as though a huge load had been lifted, leaving her light and free and drifting. 'I'm sorry,' she said. 'I'm so sleepy.'

Greg switched off the light and came back to the bed. Kneeling beside it, he took her hand in his and brushed his lips over the palm. She closed her eyes, smiling a little, and he stayed there until she slept.

In the passageway Mrs Dalton was hovering. He supposed she must have heard their raised voices a few minutes ago. It had really been quite tactful of her not to come barging into the room.

'Is she all right?'

'Asleep,' he answered briefly. He suddenly remembered that it was she who had, seemingly quite deliberately, engineered matters so that Eloise was forced to tell him about the accident. He said abruptly, 'I never got that cable. The one you sent, for Eloise.'

The genuine shock and distress on her face laid his lingering doubt to rest for ever. No one could have acted that. 'Oh, the poor baby!' she exclaimed. Her eyes filled with tears. 'She broke her heart when you didn't come, didn't even reply. I could see it, though she tried to hide it from everyone. All this time she thought you didn't care!'

'I do,' he said. 'Believe me, I do.'

'Yes,' she said hesitantly. Then, 'I haven't given you credit.'

He smiled wryly. 'I can understand that, now. No wonder you looked as though you would have liked to throw me out, when I turned up again!'

'Well ... I won't deny it. But you're Eloise's husband and ... I'm boiling the kettle again,' she said. 'Would you like some tea?'

He smiled. Her peace offering, her panacea, her pick-me-up and her only stimulant—a cup of tea. For the first time he experienced a new sensation entirely—a faint stirring of fondness for this woman who loved Eloise as much as he did, though in a quite different way. 'Thank you,' he said, although he wasn't in the least thirsty. 'I'd like that.'

The crowd in the foyer of the cinema was animated and loud. The première of *No Winners* was over, and Eloise stood beside her husband, accepting the congratulations that showered on them from all directions. Her mother had been the first to kiss them both, including Greg in her 'I'm so proud of you!' And then she and Stan stood beside their daughter and her husband, a little awed by the people who milled about waiting for their turn to tell the producer and the director and the writer what they thought of the film.

Zuleika, escorted by an ecstatic Aaron Colfax, looked like a tiger lily in flame orange and black, and the two stars, looking as much in love as they had on screen, were a focus of attention. The confirmation that Eloise and Greg were married had caused a mild stir, but rumours had been circulating for some time, and she gathered that no one was really surprised, even Isabelle, who had sulked for a few days and been difficult about her scenes, but soon recovered under the balm of Neville's determined pursuit. Much more determined than his desultory interest in herself, Eloise realised, wondering if after all he had been setting his sights on Isabelle all along.

There was a party afterwards, and at four in the morning Eloise climbed into bed and watched in some amusement as Greg prowled about the room in the half-dark, pulling off his tie, his shoes, then stopping to make a random comment on the film. 'I think it was OK,' he said. 'The kiss looked good, at the climax of the row. I thought Isabelle was going to throw something at me before we got the final take on that scene. But it did, in the end, convey the right blend of mutual anger and desire, didn't it?'

'Yes, it did.' She looked at him pensively. 'I sometimes wonder if you deliberately told her we were married just at that point in the filming, so that you could get the best performance from her. She certainly was in the mood for all that passionate fury!'

He looked at her quizzically. 'That's a bit of devious psychology that I'm afraid I'm not up to. Anyway, she was never all that interested in me, most of it was acting. She did do well in the last scene, though, didn't she? She knows her job.'

He finished undressing and slipped under the sheet beside her. With his hand on her hip, slowly caressing it, he said, 'Are you happy with it? What we've done to your book?'

'Yes, I liked it. Do you think it will do well?'

'If it doesn't, will it upset you?'

'No. I'll be disappointed for your sake, of course, but seeing the book published was my moment of triumph.'

'I'm bound to have a failure some time,' he said. 'A film that doesn't work, that the public don't like, that the critics will get out their knives for. But it won't matter, as long as I have you.'

She looked at him thoughtfully and he said, 'I know you think—thought once—that I only cared for making films. It isn't true. Why do you think I took that deadening truck-driving job?'

'I know. But you were terribly frustrated. You would have grown to hate me, and blamed me because you weren't doing what you really wanted.'

'I could never hate you.'

'Anyway, I'm glad I gave you the chance to try.'

'You didn't have to leave me to do that!'

'It seemed at the time that I did. I wanted you to have

your chance, but—I'm sorry—I didn't really believe you'd make it. I ran away from that—from watching you fail, because I couldn't have borne it. And when you asked me to go with you to America, even if you had asked me in some reasonable way, instead of throwing the offer in my face as though it were some sort of insult, I couldn't have accepted. It didn't seem right to go back to you then, when I hadn't had enough faith in you to stay while you struggled to get to the top.'

'And then, of course, I made it impossible by sounding as though I couldn't care less whether you came with me or not.'

'Did you really think I regarded you as a meal-ticket?'

'No, but I did think your parents had persuaded you that you'd married a no-hoper, and you couldn't stand the lack of security in my lifestyle. I tried to understand that. You were still very young, and I thought maybe you did need to know that I could keep you if necessary. I suppose I made it sound as though I thought you were just a mercenary little cheat. Jealousy is a very destructive emotion.'

'You didn't have any need to be jealous. I've never really looked at anyone but you.' She laughed suddenly. 'It's just my luck that every time we haven't seen each other for years, you turn up when some quite innocent man has his arms around me.'

'And it won't happen again. I've no intention of giving them the chance—innocent or otherwise.' His hand lifted one of hers, and he nibbled at her fingers. 'You're much more generous than I am. I never expected to be forgiven—even when I got back to New Zealand and instantly realised that you still felt something besides hatred for me.'

'Instantly?'

'Yes. Maybe you could have hidden it if you'd had warning. Later I sometimes doubted my own senses. But in that first moment, when I saw you standing there under the tree, even those awful coloured lights couldn't disguise the look in your eyes. When you disappeared from the party I panicked. I was scared stiff I'd never find you again.'

'Is that why you came after me?'

'Of course, and when I touched you and saw how you reacted, I knew I was right. Incredible as it seemed, you still wanted me. But the first thing you said was a reminder that you hadn't forgotten ...'

'It wasn't meant to be,' she said swiftly. 'My subconscious, perhaps.'

'Still, I knew you were holding that episode against me—not surprisingly. I was determined to follow up any advantage of surprise that I had. So I crowded you that night, out of sheer, stupid fright. I could see you'd been thrown off balance, and I didn't want to give you time to recover from it and start remembering that you hated me.'

'It might have helped if you'd said you were sorry, then!'

'*Then?* It—does this sound stupid?—it didn't seem the right moment to rake it up. Apart from the obvious fact that saying 'sorry' for something like that is totally inadequate. And I'd already told you at the time how hellishly sorry I was. I've said it so often now the words seem meaningless, but that doesn't make it less true.'

He had expressed his regret at the time, forcing the words through clenched teeth, his eyes tightly shut against what even then she had recognised were tears of remorse. But Eloise, bruised and violated and vindictive, had felt only a remote, cold satisfaction that as soon as his rage had spent itself, he was sickened by his own actions. She refused to make things easy for him. She wouldn't let him help her dress, or get her anything, just kept repeating dully, and at last almost hysterically,

'Go away. I never want to see you again. I'll never, never forgive you!' And it was true that she wouldn't have listened if he had tried to apologise again.

Greg said, 'That night when you let me make love to you at last, I thought it was going to be all right. I was grateful that I'd been allowed to wipe out the memory of the other time. Afterwards I realised I'd got it all wrong again, that you were so disgusted with yourself for giving in, you'd backtrack just as fast as you could, cover up and try to pretend it had never happened. For weeks—months—I tried to be patient, but it was a bit late.'

'Patient?' she said derisively. 'I thought you'd lost interest altogether!'

'You *couldn't* have believed that!' He dropped the hand he still held in his, and stared at her.

'Why not? You were ignoring me. There was Zuleika and Isabelle . . .'

'*Zuleika?*' His voice rose disbelievingly.

'You're not the only one who gets jealous, you know,' Eloise said tartly. 'As a matter of fact . . .'

'Yes?' he prompted.

'Well . . .' She looked embarrassed. 'You know, in my book the wife has that animosity towards the husband's comrades in arms, and eventually it's obvious that she resents everything about the war, and his fascination with the idea of heroism and patriotism, all the rest of it?'

'Yes. I know. I hope it's in the film, too.'

'The thing is . . . I didn't realise it at the time, but since doing the script, I've wondered if perhaps that's how I felt about your film-making. That it was so important in your life, it was in some way my rival. I think maybe that was one reason why I left. It was nice to tell myself that I was being rather noble, but deep down perhaps I was also trying to punish you, because I couldn't bear to play second fiddle to your career. I hated not being first.'

'You were always first. The only reason I've been able to do so well with films is that at the back of my mind I was trying to impress you.'

'The only reason?' She raised her brows sceptically.

'And the fact that I love doing it. There are other things I love doing, too.' His hand moved insinuatingly. 'Mostly with you.'

She smiled, but held him off for a moment. 'I have something to tell you,' she said.

Greg looked at her narrowly, then smiled back, and moved his hand to touch her cheek. 'I think I can guess. You're sure?'

'It isn't the first time, you know, so I recognised the symptoms.' She looked at him a little anxiously. 'Do you mind?'

'Mind?' He smiled, then laughed. 'There's some champagne in the fridge, the real stuff, left over from the party. Are you allowed some?'

She laughed. 'I don't need champagne. As long as you're pleased. You wouldn't have been, when we were first married. I think you'd have felt trapped—and jealous.'

She could see he wanted to deny it, but he admitted, 'You may be right. But I've changed since then. Of course I'm pleased. I'm delighted, thrilled, over the moon, all of that, and more.' He hugged her close and rubbed his cheek against hers, then leaned back a little, smiling. 'You're thrilled, aren't you?'

'Of course. And I'm so glad that this time you'll be here.'

'You can count on it.' His hands tightened a little as a fleeting expression of pain crossed his face.

She put her arms about him and kissed him, his lips immediately moving over hers in passionate response.

'Is it all right?' he whispered, his hands shaping her shoulders, feeling the silky warmth of her skin.

'Perfectly all right,' she assured him. Her arms were round him, and she sighed and moved against his body invitingly. He would be gentle.

He kissed her deeply, then raised his head, and bent again to touch his lips to her throat. He laughed, contentedly. 'I can hardly believe this,' he said. 'After that first night when I met you again, and you turned on me next morning, I thought that's it, I played it wrong and I've lost her for good this time. And look at me now.' He placed a warm hand on her breast, and smiled into her eyes. 'A winner, after all.'

Eloise smiled back. 'No,' she said. 'Winning implies there's a loser, and I haven't lost. In love and in war, there are no winners.'

'All right,' he said. 'Argue about the words as much as you like. You're the wordsmith. But I feel like a winner. And my field is action, not words. So kiss me and be quiet.'

Eloise laughed, pulled his hair until he firmly removed her hands and held them in his, and as he moved his mouth invitingly close to hers, raised her head a little and generously surrendered.

Harlequin Presents

Coming Next Month

Available in September wherever paperback books are sold, or through
Harlequin Reader Service:

In the U.S.
901 Fuhrmann Blvd.
P.O. Box 1397
Buffalo, N.Y. 14240-1397

In Canada
P.O. Box 603
Fort Erie, Ontario
L2A 5X3

bite of cold air that made her shiver, and she remembered that she had left her hat behind. Nothing would persuade her to return into that room again, she decided, so she turned up the collar of her coat as she ran down the four shallow steps that led to the gravel drive. She did not know how she would get back to London, but that did not matter. She would not let Luke see her crying.

CHAPTER ELEVEN

THERE was an icy patch on the bottom of the four steps that Kate did not see as she put her foot on it, and the sole of her boot slipped. She felt her ankle twist and then she was thrown forward to lurch heavily on to the gravel, flinging her hands out in front of her as she tried desperately to break her fall.

The drive rose before her alarmed eyes and then she was down. Winded, shocked, she lay where she had fallen for a moment, fighting to get her breath and feeling the stones sharp against her hands and knees. It was a temptation just to lie where she had fallen and never get up again, but she gritted her teeth and pushed herself into a sitting position, crying out when she moved her left leg and then reaching for her injured ankle to huddle over it like a wounded animal.

'It's all right . . . it's all right . . .' Suddenly he was beside her, kneeling on the gravel, his arms reaching out for her, and she choked back a gasp of anguish as he tried to help her to stand.

'Leave me alone!' The words sounded so childish that she grimaced at her own foolishness, but he ignored the command and raised her to her feet, swinging her off the ground and into his arms, and cursing softly as her injured foot bumped against his body and she stiffened in pain.

'This might not have happened if you hadn't been wearing such damn silly boots!' He sounded irritable, but she ached too much to care and his arms were a haven against her pain and her despair. It was a relief to be laid on the big chesterfield in the living room, but there was no hiding from the exasperation in his face. 'I'll give you a brandy,' he said coolly. 'Back in a minute.'

She wanted to explain that it had been an accident, and that she had dressed to please him, but what was the point? He would not understand. When he had left the room she struggled into a more upright position and stared in dismay at her muddy dress and at her holed and laddered tights that barely covered her bruised and bleeding knees. She examined her hands, wincing at the stinging pain of the gravel grazes that covered the palms, but when she tried to unzip her left boot, the pain made her feel sick.

'I'll do that. You lie quiet.' Luke was back beside her, a glass in his hand. 'Drink this and let me look at you.'

Her hand shook as she took the glass, but he seemed not to notice and his face was expressionless as he crouched by her side and eased away the boot. His head was within reach of her free hand. It seemed impossible to her that she had once had the freedom to run her fingers over it and stroke the fair silkiness, and that her touch had been welcomed.

'Your ankle does look swollen.' Gentle fingers, surprisingly gentle fingers that belied the grudging tone of his voice, ran over it, 'But I don't think you've broken anything.' The hands continued their careful exploration, but to Kate's starved senses, they were like a caress.

'You should have been a doctor,' she said, as lightly as she could manage.

'My mother's always telling me that.' He pulled

at the remnants of her tights until her foot was bare. 'Didn't I tell you that my pop's a surgeon? And my young brother's a vet.'

'No. Distinguished family.'

'You could say that.' He let her foot rest gently against the couch again. 'I think you've just sprained it,' he said.

'It may be "just sprained", but it hurts like hell!' she told him crossly.

'Until I saw it, I thought you were faking.'

'Oh, Luke, really!'

'Sorry,' he shrugged.

How was she to get home now? Wryly she did not blame him for wondering if she was really hurt. She seemed to have trapped herself most effectively in his house for the night and she knew she had to make some effort to leave.

'If you'll call me a taxi . . .' she began.

'Didn't you drive here?'

'No. Just as well.'

'I see.' What was going on behind that bland expression? How easy it would be to reach out and touch his face, that dear face that she still loved so much. It was only something in the way his eyebrows were slanted that stopped her. What was he thinking about?

'Your hands don't look too good,' he said, eyeing them. 'You'd better come upstairs and wash them.'

'Thank you.' Gritting her teeth, Kate swung her legs to the floor and, using the arm of the couch, levered herself to her feet. 'Ouch!' She could not prevent the exclamation of pain.

'Okay,' Luke sounded resigned, 'I'll carry you.'

'I'd hate to put you to so much trouble.' Now he was bringing out the very worst in her. She

knew that she sounded waspish and she felt
irritated by the clipped, unwilling offer.

He took no notice, and once again she was lifted
off her feet and again she put her arms around his
neck. It was like embracing a statue that had been
warmed by the sun, and although his arms held
her safely, that was all. His impersonality chilled
her.

Was this the man whom she had watched as he
lay sleeping, not wanting to wake him, but
impatient for the sound of his voice and the touch
of his hands? When he had opened his eyes she
remembered how he had smiled sleepily at her, and
how her heart had lurched as he had drawn her
down to him with whispered words of love.

'May I have a bath?' They were almost at the
top of the stairs.

'What? Well, I suppose so.'

The request had obviously nonplussed him, but
Kate knew she would feel better if her ankle was
soaked in warm water, and it might also help her
hands and knees.

'Maybe I should drive you home instead.' He
sounded uncertain.

'I wouldn't dream of troubling you.' He set her
on her feet and she grasped hold of the door frame
to support herself. 'Just let me clean myself up and
I'll get a taxi.'

'I think I should.' He sounded as if he had made
up his mind, and did not like the decision he had
come to.

'Luke ...' Standing on one foot, reminding
herself of an uncertain stork, Kate laid a hand on
his arm and looked up at him, '... when I come
down, could we talk for a little while?'

'Oh, Kate!'

'Please!' She tightened her grip on his arm, seeing his indecision but sensing that if she pressed him, he would agree. 'Please,' she said again.

'All right.' He shrugged indifferently. 'Do you want something to eat?'

'No, thank you.'

'Coffee?'

'That would be nice.' If he was polite for very much longer she would either scream or shake him until he lost that unnatural calm.

'Call me when you're ready.' He turned and stalked away, straight-backed, probably already regretting his decision to talk to her, but Kate had got what she wanted and she was satisfied for the moment.

After a long wallow in the warmth of the water she dried herself leisurely and found herself smiling as she did so. Events had unexpectedly gone her way, and in the bath she had enjoyed a respite to work out the best way of taking advantage of the situation, the best way to approach him. Now, as she opened the bathroom door, she knew how to do it. The pain in her ankle had eased and she felt relaxed and confident.

She descended the stairs slowly, one step at a time, trying to keep the weight off her left leg, her bare feet making no sound on the thick carpet, and she was only two steps from the bottom when Luke came out of a door to her left, a cigar between his lips. He stopped and stared at her, and with a slight lift of her eyebrows, Kate looked straight back at him.

'What's all this, then?' he asked softly.

'My dress is muddy. I can't wear it.'

'You're expecting me to take you back like that?'

Allowing a hint of a smile to cross her face, she shook her head slightly, but her eyes never left his.

'It'll be dry soon,' she told him.

'How's your ankle?'

'Better, I think. But if you'd give me a hand . . .' Her voice trailed off.

'Of course.' He stepped forward and helped her to descend the last two stairs, then, 'Isn't this all rather theatrical?' he asked.

'I don't know what you mean.'

'No?'

He would have to be very, very naïve not to understand what she was doing and to guess why she was doing it. They both knew that, but he humoured her by taking her arm and letting her lean on him as she limped into the living room, where he settled her, with a show of solicitude that made her smile, on to the chesterfield which he had drawn closer to the fire. He obviously intended letting her continue the masquerade for a little while.

Coffee was put on a small table and brought close to her elbow, he lit her cigarette, then sat in the chair on the other side of the fireplace and they looked at one another.

'You wanted to talk,' Luke prompted quietly. 'What about?'

'You and me.'

'I think that's ungrammatical, but we'll let it pass. What did you want to say?'

Kate fiddled with the belt of her robe and refused to look at him. What did she want to say? When it came down to the basic question she simply did not know. And did it really matter? If he no longer loved her then all the words in the world would not help her now. What was the

point of trying to make him understand how she
felt when he really did not care?

'I'd like to go home,' she said.

'Why?'

Was he not going to allow her any pride?

'Because.'

'Because you know you were wrong to run out
on me the way you did, or because you're too
proud to say you're sorry and really mean it?'

That hurt. She raised her head and looked into
eyes that were as stormy as the sea she loved so
much. Gone was the blandness and the indiffer-
ence. Now his face was as vital and alive as it had
been during those blissful four days. There was no
laughter in those beloved features, but anything
was better than the bleak calm that she had been
watching earlier.

'I was wrong,' she said gently. 'And I'm sorry.
So very sorry.'

'So am I.' His voice whispered its message
through the hush of the room and she frowned as
she tried to interpret its meaning. He had nothing
to be sorry for.

'Luke . . .' She said his name and then stopped.
The speeches that she had prepared in the bath to
relate to him had disappeared. All the carefully
constructed explanations had vanished and she felt
vulnerable without the protection of words.
Hadn't they been her whole life? And yet now,
when she needed them so desperately, she had
nothing left to say. All her world was wrapped up
in that one simple name, but how could she expect
him to understand that?

'What, my love?'

My love? He had called her 'my love'! Surely it
had slipped out without him realising what he had

said? Her eyes widened and her fingers slipped nervelessly from the sash around her waist.

'What did you call me?' she asked incredulously.

'My love.' His eyebrows arched. 'So?'

'A minute ago you'd hardly talk to me . . .'

'Yeah, I know.' He rubbed his hand over his hair and seemed almost embarrassed. 'Stupid, isn't it?'

'I don't understand,' Kate said faintly.

'Right now I'm not too sure that I do.'

'There's so much I want to explain to you . . .' she spread out her hands in a gesture of appeal, '. . . but I just can't. All the words are inside my head, but they won't come out.'

'You don't have to explain.' He stretched out his hand and for the first time, Kate saw her own manuscript on a small table. 'I've been reading this again tonight. It's all there, isn't it? All the reasons why you wouldn't come to the States.'

'That's just a story.'

'No, it isn't. It's my love-letter.'

'What?' She stared at him disbelievingly. 'Luke, what are you talking about?'

'I'm talking about the lonely little girl who grew up with just her imagination for a companion, who was allowed to run loose over the countryside because her parents were too busy on their farm. I'm talking about the girl who grew into a woman and knew that she had to be independent because she didn't dare to trust anyone enough to love them. She met one man she could love, but he didn't understand, so she ran away. Thank God. Then she met another man and he was just as blind. Only he came to his senses in the end.' He paused and smiled, and Kate's heart flipped over.

'You're reading something into that book that

isn't there!' she protested weakly.

'No? You just didn't realise what you were writing.'

'That book is fiction.'

'That book is fact.'

Impasse. She glared at him, but her mind was busy running over the plot of her novel, looking for parallels with her own life. And finding them. Why had she not realised? Bewildered by his sudden change of mood, she dropped her gaze to stare at the pattern of the Indian carpet on the floor.

'I read some of it while you were in the bath,' Luke continued, and now his voice was so gentle that she wanted to cry. 'I hadn't realised till then just how vulnerable you are underneath that tough exterior. You tried to tell me, didn't you? At the cottage the night it got vandalised, but I didn't understand you.'

'This is all wrong . . .'

'No it isn't.' He rose swiftly and she panicked, not sure of his intentions, pressing herself against the back of the chesterfield in a defensive action that she was sure he would not miss. 'I know Kate Fisher now.' He crouched down in front of her and his eyes were very blue and very direct. 'I thought I knew her before, but I was wrong. I thought everything had to be done Kate's way. Now I know that my beautiful Kate's just been waiting for someone to come along who can prove to her that he's stronger than she is.'

'I didn't realise that you were a psychologist.' She could feel the veneer of her confidence crumbling beneath his watching eyes and she was grateful for the hands that suddenly reached out and covered hers. 'It isn't like that at all. I don't need anyone to tell me what to do!'

'No?' The grip of his hands tightened. 'Are you sure? You better think about it, my love. Do you want a life living out of suitcases . . . being on your own . . . until that shell of toughness you've made for yourself becomes a part of you? Or would you rather come back to the States with me?'

'Luke . . .' She wasn't hearing him correctly. She couldn't be.

'I've never seen you so lost for words before.' He was smiling now and, confused, Kate lowered her gaze to watch his thumb caress the bones of her wrist. 'Isn't this what you want?' he asked. 'You and me. Like this. For always?'

'Luke . . .' She had to find something to say. Something, anything was better than this repeating of his name like a dazed parrot. The simile pleased her and she smiled.

'What?' He seemed to be waiting for something. 'Why are you smiling?'

'Nothing, really. I just don't think I believe any of this.'

'Believe it, babe. I'm still hooked on you. The past doesn't matter.' He was dismissing it with a wave of his hand, but she was still not sure that she should let it rest there. He was confusing her, both with his physical presence and by what he was saying, and she could not think straight.

Restlessly she shifted on the chesterfield and caught her breath as her injured ankle protested at the sudden movement. She looked down at it.

'I don't think I'm going to be able to get my boot back on,' she told him. 'My ankle's swelling.' She needed a diversion. Needed a few moments to sort out all the statements he was making.

Luke shrugged. 'We both know you're not going back tonight, so why worry?'

'We do?' She tried to look innocent.

'Sure we do. Would you come downstairs in a bathrobe several inches too short for you, with bare feet and your hair piled up in that silly, endearing topknot, if you'd intended going away? There's a mirror in the bathroom. You must have known what you looked like.'

Of course she had known. She had been pleased with the effect and grateful to the owner of the robe for being several inches shorter than she was.

'I thought it looked rather nice,' she agreed demurely.

'Nice is not the word I'd have used. Were you planning to seduce me?' His finger ran along the line of her jaw and trailed slowly down to her throat. 'Would you really have gone before you slipped over?'

'Yes. Would you have let me?'

'I don't know. Maybe.' His hand reached upwards to stroke across her hairline. 'But I'd have come after you in the end.'

'I cried a lot in Devon.' Now his fingers were tracing the shape of her ear and she shivered. 'I didn't just hurt you, you know. I missed you so badly. And I've got all your records now.'

'That's nice.' Luke grinned like a schoolboy. 'So why didn't you call me? I might have yelled, but I'd have come.'

'I thought I could get over you.' Kate became aware that they had slipped away from the central issue and were fencing with one another like uncertain duellists. 'It took me a long time to learn that I wasn't going to.'

'Why won't you answer my question?' He reached for her hand and pressed a kiss into her palm.

'What question?'

'Don't be stupid, Kate. I want you to come back to the States with me. Will you?'

They stared at one another, conversely held together and separated by memories of the past.

'What are you waiting for?' He was so close, so impossibly close. Couldn't he see from her face what she was going to say to him? 'Are you thinking about what I said to you at the party? I'm sorry, love. That was my male pride talking. I got thrown off balance when Tony told me you were there and I wanted to make you pay for hurting me. What fools we are, sweetheart!'

Kate smiled then, touched by his rueful voice and the small kisses with which he was covering her fingers. Yet she still had not given him an answer and the tension was beginning to build between them, slowly and quietly, feeding on a last uncertainty that she could resolve with just a few simple words, although, strangely, she did not feel that he was worried by her reticence. Was he so sure of her?

'I hardly recognised you at the party.' Luke stretched up and cupped his hand behind her head to fiddle with the pins that secured her hair. 'You looked so sophisticated and cool and confident. I thought maybe you'd come to show me that you didn't care about me. It was the same tonight. You were like a stranger. But I know the girl with the bare feet and the skimpy bathrobe.'

He began to pull the pins out, and when her hair tumbled down around her shoulders he began to thread his fingers through it.

'This is my Kate.' There was great satisfaction in his voice and he sat back on his heels to see her better. Then, 'I prefer it shorter.'

'I'll get it cut tomorrow.'

'I believe you would!'

Yes, she would if he really wanted her to. Surely he knew that? And did he also not realise that he had not mentioned love in either of his requests for her to return to the States with him? Was it a deliberate omission or did he just take it for granted that she knew how he felt?

'I'll come back with you.' She had to be with him. Some of the old doubts still lingered, but she would just have to fight them. With or without his help.

'Kate, I love you!' Luke spoke softly, but he emphasised each word as if it was a kind of promise. 'Come here . . .' and then he was leaning forward to put a hand behind her head and draw her towards him.

He took his time, seeming to savour the moment, and she saw his face coming closer and shut her eyes as his lips touched hers lightly, just for a moment. Butterfly kiss. Not enough, not nearly enough. She opened her mouth to protest, but then he was kissing her desperately, achingly, and her fingers curved around his shoulders to hold him closer, giving herself up to his strength.

'I want to marry you . . .' He spoke against her mouth, kissing the corners of her lips gently but still holding her so tightly that she could hardly breathe. Her body stiffened in surprise.

'You don't have to.' She felt she had to tell him that for the sake of her conscience, but she buried her face into his neck so that he would not see the hope in her eyes.

'Yes, I do. Because of what and who you are. I have to keep you safe, my love. You won't be happy any other way. And I guess I'm selfish enough to want to be sure of you. We have the right kind of love. I want to marry you.'

'You aren't capable of selfishness.' She stroked the nape of his neck with one finger, gently and lovingly.

'And you haven't given me an answer yet.' His fingers turned her face so that she had to look at him, and he scanned it with the faint beginnings of a frown on his own. 'There's something going on in that busy brain of yours,' he teased her. 'Something complicated. Tell me.'

'I want the answers to some questions.'

'Oh God, no!' His groan was deliberately theatrical. 'Can't you leave it alone, my love? Can't you understand that I know why you never came to the States? Even when I cursed you for making a fool out of me, I hoped that one day you'd find a man you could really trust . . .'

'Shh!' She laid her fingers over his lips and smiled at the frustration in his eyes. 'We can talk about that later. Just tell me one thing . . .'

'No wonder they call the British the bulldog breed!' Luke broke away long enough to say the words and then obediently replaced her fingers over his lips, his eyes alight with laughter.

'Oh, Luke!' He was not going to be serious. He was going to infuriate her with his impish, irresistible humour. 'Why didn't you ask me to marry you when you were at the cottage with me?'

The laughter faded. He looked wary. Kate removed her fingers and waited for his answer, her head tilted on one side and her hands folded patiently in her lap.

'I . . .' He seemed lost for words. Abruptly he got to his feet and went over to stand by the fire, fiddling absentmindedly with a small ornamental silver frog. Then he turned to face her. 'It was a mistake,' he admitted. 'But I did have a reason. I knew how independent you were . . . or I thought I did. I reckoned maybe the idea of marriage might scare you. So I thought I'd get you over to the States and make things so good for you that when I did ask you, you wouldn't be able to turn me down. If I'd asked you in England and you'd said no, well . . .' he shrugged, 'I didn't have enough time to wait around and get you to change your mind.'

Kate deliberately made no answer to that statement for a few moments. Then she held his gaze and spoke softly;

'That tells me such a lot. I thought you were sure of me.'

'No.'

'You didn't trust me enough to tell me how you really felt.'

His head had been down as he studied the ornament within his hands. He lifted it to stare at her but, quietly confident, she simply smiled as she watched the expressions flickering across his mobile face. He wanted to deny what she had said. It wasn't true. Then she saw the acceptance of her truth and finally the wry smile that said it all.

'Okay.' Luke put down the frog and held up his hands in mock surrender. 'I give in. You've backed me into a corner. I was just as scared as you . . . just as vulnerable.'

'And I didn't understand,' she told him softly. 'Come here, love.'

He came towards her swiftly and compulsively, sure of his welcome within her arms.

'If only we'd been honest . . .'

'Hush, love, it's over now.' His face buried itself against her throat and his arms imprisoned and comforted her. She stroked his hair gently and stared into the heart of the fire. Later she would tell him all about Miles, make him really understand all the doubts and fears that had been inside her head during those four days.

'You still haven't said yes,' he reminded her.

'You haven't asked me,' she retorted swiftly. 'Not properly.'

She had been leaning against the back of the chesterfield, taking the weight of the upper part of his body against her own and her arms locked around his shoulders. When she spoke, he pushed himself away from her abruptly, and his face was clouded as he stared at her.

'Hey, this won't do! Yes or no, Kate. No thinking about it and no maybes. I want to know and I want to know now!'

'And I thought you were so romantic!' she sighed.

'Kate!' His voice threatened.

'I'm teasing,' she told him softly. 'The answer is yes. Did you honestly think . . .'

'Brat!'

Blue eyes, hazy with love, smiled into hers, and then she was being pushed back again as his mouth sought hers with a passion that was so much a part of what he was.

For nine months all she had survived on was memories, and now these seemed such an

insubstantial shadow compared to the reality.
Now she no longer had to control her eagerness
for him. His mouth demanded her surrender
and at the same time begged to be shown the
length and breadth of her love, and now there
was no room for anything but wholehearted
response.

She gave him all that he asked for and more,
knowing with a feeling of heady certainty that she
could be what he wanted. The brittle, protective
shell of independence was breaking into melting
shards of ice around her, and for the first time in
her life she felt free. Luke had done this, and
joyously she ran her hands down his back to slip
them beneath his sweater and feel the warmth of
his body through his shirt as she held him closer
still. She was slipping into that familiar vortex
where love and desire and need spiralled her into a
world where no coherent thought, no logical idea
was possible, and it was Luke who finally raised
his head.

'I have to go to New York in two days,' he said
quietly.

'Luke!'

'Sorry, babe.'

'You're impossible! Is it always going to be like
this?'

'I'm going to be moving around a lot for a few
years anyway. Will you be able to cope with it?'

It wouldn't always be easy for them. Kate
recognised that. His profession would give them
more difficulties than most people in love would
have to bear. Yet she would be with him. Together
they could make their marriage work.

'I'm sure I will,' she whispered, and his lips took
hers again in gentle gratitude.

Later—whether it was hours or minutes Kate neither knew nor cared—she was brought back to the present as Luke laughed softly.

'Something funny?' she asked, wanting to share every one of his thoughts. She was sitting curled up on his lap in the big chair in front of the fire, head contentedly nestled against his shoulder but tilted back a little so that she could see his face and exchange kisses with him.

'Not really,' he answered her honestly. 'I was just thinking that I'd got everything I want right here . . . and then I remembered I hadn't got quite all I want.'

'The film rights? You really want them so badly?' she tugged gently at his thick hair.

'There's things I want more at the moment.' His eyes told her exactly what he wanted, and she remembered seeing the same expression in them before, at her cottage all those months ago.

His mouth hovered mutely over hers and she kissed him lightly and fleetingly, teasing him, playing a game that was familiar to both of them.

'Love, I'm trying to be serious,' she protested.

'You're trying to drive me out of my skull and succeeding very nicely. You talk too much.'

His grumbling was goodnatured, but now she did not want to play games either, and the fingers that had pulled at his hair opened as she drew him down to kiss her, giving herself up to what he wanted and what she could not live without.

There was just one more thing she had to say, one gesture she had to make to show him that her confidence and trust in him was absolute.

'Luke,' she said. 'Luke!'

'What is it now?'

'The film rights . . .'

'You mean my love-letter?'

'Would you like them as a wedding present? I don't know what Niall will say, but . . .'

His kiss was black velvet laced with white lightning. Kate surrendered to it willingly and gave herself up to loving and being loved. Luke's way.

Coming Next Month in Harlequin Romance!

2629 A GIRL CALLED ANDY   Rosemary Badger
A tempestuous romance about a young teacher trying to
forge a life for herself and her younger siblings in
Tasmania—without the interference of her autocratic
neighbor, a handsome novelist.

2630 MAELSTROM   Ann Cooper
An arrogant oil executive believes that Samantha, a British
engineer, has no place in Saudi Arabia—except perhaps in
his bed! Samantha tries heroically to resist his charm and
prove him wrong.

2631 THE CHEQUERED SILENCE   Jacqueline Gilbert
A young actress deserts her man—a famous director—for
reasons she fears to divulge. When they meet again years
later, he still cannot forgive her—nor can she reveal her
secret....

2632 DESERT FLOWER   Dana James
Two British doctors, one an opinionated male and the other
a beautiful woman, fight for their different points of view—
and fight against their mutual attraction—in an Egyptian
oasis clinic.

2633 ONCE MORE WITH FEELING   Natalie Spark
Life becomes unbearably complicated for a young English
actress when she performs in a play directed by her one-time
idol, a man who years before humiliated her—and betrayed
her actress mother!

2634 ALMOST A STRANGER   Margaret Way
Sydney, Australia, is the setting for this intriguing love story
of a young woman caught in a family feud—and caught in
the throes of desire for a man she finds just too disturbing....

Harlequin Photo ~Calendar~

Turn Your Favorite Photo into a Calendar.

JULY 1984

The Browns

Uniquely yours, this 10 x 17½" calendar features your favorite photograph, with any name you wish in attractive lettering at the bottom. A delightfully personal and practical idea!

Send us your favorite color print, black-and-white print, negative, or slide, any size (we'll return it), along with **3** proofs of purchase (coupon below) from a June or July release of Harlequin Romance, Harlequin Presents, Harlequin Superromance, Harlequin American Romance or Harlequin Temptation, plus $5.75 (includes shipping and handling).

Share the joys and sorrows of real-life love with
Harlequin American Romance!™.

GET THIS BOOK
FREE as your introduction to
Harlequin American Romance —
an exciting series of romance
novels written especially for
the American woman of today.

Mail to:
Harlequin Reader Service

In the U.S.
2504 West Southern Ave.
Tempe, AZ 85282

In Canada
P.O. Box 2800, Postal Station A
5170 Yonge St., Willowdale, Ont. M2N 5T5

YES! I want to be one of the first to discover
Harlequin American Romance. Send me FREE and without
obligation *Twice in a Lifetime.* If you do not hear from me after I
have examined my FREE book, please send me the 4 new
Harlequin American Romances each month as soon as they
come off the presses. I understand that I will be billed only $2.25
for each book (total $9.00). There are no shipping or handling
charges. There is no minimum number of books that I have to
purchase. In fact, I may cancel this arrangement at any time.
Twice in a Lifetime is mine to keep as a FREE gift, even if I do not
buy any additional books. 154 BPA **NAVD**

Name	(please print)

Address	Apt. no.

City	State/Prov.	Zip/Postal Code

Signature (If under 18, parent or guardian must sign.)

AMR-SUB-1

Discover the new and unique

Harlequin Gothic and Regency Romance Specials!

Gothic Romance	Regency Romance
THE CASTLE AT JADE COVE Helen Hicks	A GENTLEMAN'S AGREEMENT Deborah Lynne
AN INNOCENT MADNESS Dulcie Hollyock	REVENGE FOR A DUCHESS Sara Orwig
RESTLESS OBSESSION Jane Toombs	MIDNIGHT FOLLY Phyllis Pianka

A new and exciting world of romance reading

Harlequin Gothic and Regency Romance Specials!